"Do you believe in destiny, Meggy?"

Margaret closed her eyes. "I don't know," she whispered.

"I do," Caleb said. "I believe some things are preordained. No matter what we do, or how we struggle against them, they're meant to happen."

"Caleb—"

"That's what I think happened with us," he continued determinedly, just as if she hadn't spoken. "I think we were destined to meet. I also think we're destined to have dinner together tonight."

Pushing away the impossible yearning that filled her, Margaret said, "I'm sorry, Caleb. I can't."

"Ahh, sweet Meggy, of course you can. It's easy. All you have to do is say yes...."

Dear Reader,

Welcome to Silhouette **Special Edition**...welcome
to romance.

The lazy, hazy days and nights of August are perfect
for romantic summer stories. These wonderful books
are sure to take your mind off the heat but still warm
your heart.

This month's THAT SPECIAL WOMAN! selection is
by Rita Award-winner Cheryl Reavis. *One of Our Own*
takes us to the hot plains of Northern Arizona for a tale
of destiny and love, as a family comes together in the
land of the Navajo.

And this month also features two exciting spin-offs
from favorite authors. Erica Spindler returns with
Baby, Come Back, her follow-up to *Baby Mine,*
and Pamela Toth tells Daniel Sixkiller's story in
The Wedding Knot—you first met Daniel in Pamela's
last Silhouette **Special Edition** novel, *Walk Away, Joe.*
And not to be missed are terrific books by Lucy Gordon,
Patricia McLinn and Trisha Alexander.

I hope you enjoy this book, and the rest of the summer!

Sincerely,

Tara Gavin
Senior Editor

Please address questions and book requests to:
Silhouette Reader Service
U.S.: 3010 Walden Ave., P.O. Box 1325, Buffalo, NY 14269
Canadian: P.O. Box 609, Fort Erie, Ont. L2A 5X3

TRISHA ALEXANDER

WHAT WILL THE CHILDREN THINK?

Silhouette®

SPECIAL EDITION®

Published by Silhouette Books
America's Publisher of Contemporary Romance

This book is dedicated to the greatest high school graduating class ever—the Struthers (Ohio) High Shool Class of 1954. Thanks for forty wonderful years of memories.
Special thanks to the best writing buddies on earth: Heather Allison, Alaina Hawthorne, Carla Luan, Sue Royer and Amanda Stevens.

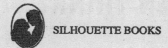 SILHOUETTE BOOKS

ISBN 0-373-09906-1

WHAT WILL THE CHILDREN THINK?

This edition published by arrangement with Harlequin Enterprises B. V.

® and TM are trademarks of Harlequin Enterprises B. V., used under license. Trademarks indicated with ® are registered in the United States Patent and Trademark Office, the Canadian Trade Marks Office and in other countries.

Printed in U.S.A.

Books by Trisha Alexander

Silhouette Special Edition

Cinderella Girl #640
When Somebody Loves You #748
When Somebody Needs You #784
Mother of the Groom #801
When Somebody Wants You #822
Here Comes the Groom #845
Say You Love Me #875
What Will the Children Think? #906

TRISHA ALEXANDER

has had a lifelong love affair with books and always wanted to be a writer. She also loves cats, movies, the ocean, music, Broadway shows, cooking, traveling, being with her family and friends, Cajun food, "Calvin and Hobbes" and getting mail. Trisha and her husband have three grown children, two adorable grandchildren, and live in Houston, Texas. Trisha loves to hear from readers. You can write to her at P.O. Box 441603, Houston, TX 77244-1603.

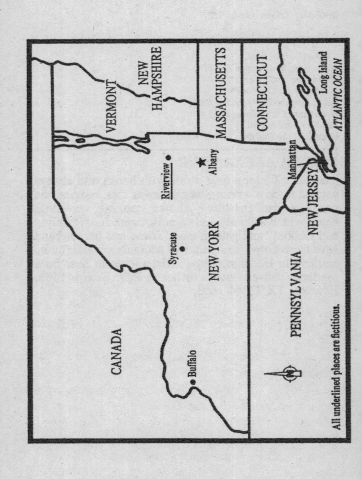

All undelined places are fictitious.

Chapter One

Come live with me, and be my love,
And we will some new pleasures prove...
　　　　　　　　　　　　　—John Donne

"*M*o-ther! I need my *sweatshirts!* What's *taking* you so long?"

Margaret Desmond hurried to the bottom of the stairwell. The strident voice calling from upstairs belonged to her youngest daughter, Lori, who was packing prior to leaving for the fall semester at Riverview College.

"I'm coming, I'm coming," Margaret mumbled. Arms full of the warm laundry she'd just finished folding, she hastily climbed the curved staircase leading to the second floor of her spacious Colonial-style home.

"I'm gonna be late!" Lori complained, a petulant expression flitting across her pretty, oval-shaped face. The gray eyes she'd inherited from her father, so lovely at times, now reflected irritation and impatience. "I thought you were coming *with* me," she said crossly, flipping her blond hair back. Snatching the folded clothing from Margaret's arms, Lori began stuffing the additional items into the open suitcase sitting on top of her bed.

Margaret told herself to be patient. She told herself Lori was just nervous about starting her first semester in college. She told herself her daughter did not mean to sound so critical. "I *am* coming with you," she said quietly.

Lori reached for her hair dryer. She plunked it on top of the items in the suitcase, then slammed the lid shut. Her gaze swept Margaret. "In *that?*"

Margaret looked down at her clothing. She wore a belted, green striped shirtwaist dress and matching green pumps. "What's wrong with this?"

Lori shrugged. "It's just orientation, Mother. You didn't have to get dressed up."

Margaret sighed. "Honey, I'm forty-five years old. I'm your mother. People expect mothers to dress up."

Lori shrugged again.

Margaret wanted to cry, *What happened to the little girl who used to think I was wonderful, who used to think everything I did was right? Why is it that suddenly, in the past few years, and especially in the eight months since your father died, everything I do is wrong?*

But saying these things wouldn't have done any good. Lori would have simply given Margaret another of her exasperated looks. Sadly, Margaret and Lori no longer seemed able to communicate. Margaret could only hope this was a temporary condition. That someday she and Lori might have as good a relationship as Margaret had with her oldest daughter, Lisa.

"Why don't we start loading up the car?" Margaret suggested, reaching for one of the suitcases.

Forty minutes later they were on their way. Margaret drove the Cadillac carefully. Margaret did everything carefully. Carefully and correctly.

Her best friend, Rosemary Beil, the publisher of the *Riverview Record,* the only newspaper in Riverview, New York, periodically teased Margaret about her circumspect life.

"Honestly, Margaret," she'd said as recently as a week ago, "Anthony's dead. You don't have to please anyone but yourself now. Loosen up a little bit. Live dangerously. Be the Merry Widow! You're so all-fired *proper!*"

"I can't help it," Margaret had answered glumly, knowing Rosemary was right. "I was brought up to do the right thing. I couldn't change if I wanted to."

How could she possibly explain to Rosemary that she'd love to be more daring and take more risks, but she didn't know how. Rosemary wouldn't have understood. Rosemary had always been daring. She'd always taken risks. Starting the newspaper had been a giant risk, but look at the dividends she'd reaped.

Margaret sighed and braked for a yellow light.

Lori drummed her fingers against her thigh—a thigh clad in tight-fitting designer blue jeans. "You could have made it through that light, Mother. No one else stops for yellow lights!" Her voice dripped with disgust. "I'm supposed to meet Judy in front of the dorm at one o'clock, and if we don't hurry, I'll never make it."

Margaret glanced down at her watch. "It's only twelve forty-five. We'll be there in plenty of time."

In answer, Lori only drummed her fingers harder. Then, shooting Margaret another irritated look, she reached for the radio buttons. A second later, a blast of rock music filled the car.

Margaret winced, but she didn't comment. Instead she watched the lush green landscape of Riverview roll by. The sight of Riverview, even on this hot August afternoon, should have soothed her. She had always loved this area of upstate New York—its gently rolling hills, its cool lakes and rivers, its verdant countryside—but today she felt a curious dissatisfaction.

When Anthony was alive, his position as head of the marketing department for McPhee's Medical Supply had sent him to numerous conventions and conferences throughout the United States. Margaret had generally accompanied him, and she had enjoyed the trips, but she'd always been happy to get back home to the safe and familiar in Riverview. She'd been born in the small college town, lived her entire life there, and expected to be buried there.

Several times in the past couple of months, though, Margaret had experienced an alien thought. A thought of how nice it would be to do something different. Live somewhere else. In her more sensible moments, she knew this whim was probably just a normal reaction to her widowhood and all the added responsibilities it had thrust upon her shoulders.

"Finally," Lori said, interrupting Margaret's reverie. They had reached the university. Margaret drove straight to Lori's dormitory, an attractive redbrick building nestled in a stand of silver birch trees. Even the decision that Lori would live in the women's dormitory this first year away from home had caused an argument between her and Margaret. Lori had wanted to get an apartment with two other girls. An apartment off campus.

Margaret, who was only now—all these months after Anthony's death—beginning to learn how to be firm when she had to, had calmly refused to even consider the idea. "I'm sorry, Lori," she'd said. "You can either live in the dorm this year or live at home."

Lori had chosen the dorm, as Margaret knew she would. At least in the dorm she would have some restrictions, Margaret hoped.

"There's Judy!" Lori exclaimed, and Margaret saw the pretty redhead sitting on the low concrete wall that rimmed the flower beds in front of the dorm.

"Hi, Mrs. Desmond," Judy said as Margaret pulled up in front. She got up and walked over to the car.

"Hello, Judy."

The two girls quickly unloaded Lori's things.

Twenty minutes later, with Lori's belongings stowed in her dorm room, the three of them walked over to Richardson Center, where the freshmen orientation reception was being held. Students, parents, faculty members and others clogged the entrance hall, where a long table had been set up and several administrative workers dispensed name tags and orientation packets.

While Judy and Lori lined up for their packets, Margaret moved off to the side and waited. Idly she looked around. A burst of giggles drew her attention. Down the hall a few feet away, a bunch of young women stood around a good-looking, dark-haired man, who grinned at them and gestured with his hands while he talked.

The way the young women preened and hung on his every word made Margaret smile. She was glad she wasn't that young anymore. Although, now that she took a closer look, the man they hovered around wasn't nearly as young as the young women—who were obviously students. He looked to be in his mid-to-late thirties.

As she watched, the man said something that made all the young women laugh again, then he broke away from the group and strode in Margaret's direction. Well, swaggered might be a better description of his walk, she thought. He had an air of self-confidence about him that Margaret admired every time she saw it in someone, because it was a trait she had never possessed.

As he passed, his gaze met hers. Margaret took one look into his eyes and realized exactly why he'd held those girls in thrall. He was one of the most blatantly sexy men she'd ever seen, and his eyes were so blue that looking into them was like drowning in deep ocean waters. To her amazement, he grinned at her and winked.

Flustered, Margaret looked away, and when she looked back, he was gone. Wondering who he was, she took a deep breath to steady a suddenly accelerated heartbeat. Heavens, she was acting just as silly as those young women had been. That man was obviously a big flirt, and winking at her was as natural to him as taking a breath. He probably grinned and winked at eighty-year-old ladies, too.

"Well, Margaret, is everything ready for the party Friday night?"

Margaret jumped. She turned, then smiled at the tall, sandy-haired man who had approached her. All thoughts of blue eyes and winks faded from her mind.

"Hello, Dean Anderson. Yes, everything's ready, and I'm really looking forward to it."

"Mrs. Anderson and I are looking forward to it, too. We've been hearing nice things about your business and the kind of job you're doing."

A warm rush of pleasure filled Margaret. She had started Party Line, a party-planning service, four months earlier, after twenty-seven years of being a full-time wife and mother who had never held a paying job. When she'd first decided—after Anthony's heart attack—that she had to find something to do with the rest of her life, she hadn't had any idea what that something might be. She wasn't qualified to do anything.

She had no education beyond high school, no skills, no training and no experience. She had just turned forty-five, and she felt like an anachronism in today's world. She'd about decided she'd have to go to school to learn some kind of trade or something.

Then, one afternoon, during a neighborhood coffee Ellie Liptak, Margaret's next-door neighbor, said, "You put on the *best* parties, Margaret. Do you ever hire out?" Ellie's eyes twinkled. "Doug wants me to have a dinner party for his department, and I'm *terrified!*"

Margaret had volunteered, on the spot, to take charge of Ellie's dinner party. Afterward, she couldn't believe she'd done anything quite so impulsive. The gesture turned out to have important ramifications, though, because the success of Ellie's dinner party got Margaret thinking about the fact that she actually did have some skills, after all.

Within weeks, Party Line was born. Since that day in May, Margaret's business had slowly grown, spreading by word of mouth. And two weeks ago, she'd been very pleased to get her first job at the university. Dean Anderson's wife had called her to say they wanted to give a party to celebrate the promotion of one of the English professors to head of the English Department.

"And we'd like to hire you to do the party for us," Mrs. Anderson said. "We want you to do everything. Even the food."

Margaret was thrilled. She felt this assignment was a test of sorts. If she did a good job for Dean Anderson, she might be asked to handle some of the bigger parties and receptions hosted by the university. So she'd thrown herself into the preparations. And now the big event was just two days away.

Margaret hadn't lied to Dean Anderson. Just about everything was ready. All she had left to do was to supervise the last-minute preparation of food, and that would be done at the party site.

She smiled. Anthony's death had been a shock, but she'd survived. In fact, although she had never admitted this to anyone—not even Rosemary—Margaret was beginning to like being independent. And if she could make a success out of her fledgling business, she knew she would like it even more. That's why Friday night was so important.

At four o'clock Friday afternoon Margaret carried the last of the party supplies to her van. She surveyed the items, ticking them off her list. "Six platters. Two punch bowls. Sixty cups. Coffeemaker." She made a red check mark at the last item, then carefully closed the back doors of the van.

Two hours later, Margaret stood in the kitchen of Dean Anderson's home and orchestrated the preparation of the party trays. She regularly used another woman to help her with food preparation, and for tonight's party, she'd also hired two young women to work as servers. The girls were busily arranging pinwheel sandwiches on two large crystal platters. Teresa Minchin, the cook, finished ladling potato salad into a huge bowl, then she sprinkled paprika over the top. From the oven, the tantalizing aroma of baking ham wafted through the room.

"We're nearly done," Margaret said. Everything seemed to be under control. The guests would begin arriving at seven, and all the food should be ready by then.

Margaret walked into the large combination living room/dining room. The weather had cooperated today, and the recent heat wave had abated. The French doors at the end of the living room stood open, and Margaret moved out onto the flagstone patio. A warm breeze ruffled her hair.

Everything looked perfect, she thought, glancing around. The lanterns had been strung earlier, and as soon as dusk fell, they would be lit. The potted red geraniums that rimmed the patio looked lush and beautiful, the spruce trees at the edge of the lawn were appropriately full and green, and the recently watered lawn sparkled jade under the rays of the afternoon sun. Lorraine Anderson's late-summer roses perfumed the air.

Yes, everything was ready.

One of the most important nights of Margaret's life was about to begin. She hoped nothing would go wrong.

A little before seven the first guest arrived. From then on, a steady stream followed. Margaret didn't pay much attention because she was too busy overseeing the food and bar.

By eight o'clock, much of the food needed replenishing. Margaret worked along with the servers. About ten minutes after eight, she glanced up from her task of refilling a bowl of peanuts, and looked straight into the blue eyes she'd found so arresting the first time she'd seen them at Richardson Center two days earlier.

Her heart skipped a beat and her hands stilled. For a long moment, she stared, and the man with the blue eyes stared back. Then, slowly, eyes twinkling, he winked at her again, and a smile spread across his face.

Margaret could feel herself blushing. She hurriedly looked away from those compelling eyes and that dangerous smile.

Who *was* he? she wondered as she headed back toward the kitchen. He must be an instructor. Why else would he be at this party? Margaret didn't know many of the university people. She and Anthony hadn't been a part of that circle. Their friends came from the town itself—people they'd gone to school with, people connected with Anthony's business, people from their church and their neighborhood.

"Nice party, Margaret," said a voice behind her, and Margaret turned. The woman who had spoken was one of the few university people Margaret did know. Catherine Higgins and Margaret had gone to high school together, and now Catherine taught English Literature at the university.

"Thanks, Catherine." She smiled. "I didn't see you come in."

Catherine, an attractive blonde, smiled back. "I was late. Just got here, as a matter of fact."

Margaret liked Catherine, who was down-to-earth and sensible. She hadn't seen much of her in recent years, mostly because of Anthony and his prejudice against "those eggheads," as he referred to them.

"How have you been?" Catherine asked.

"I'm doing well."

"Adjusting to life alone okay?"

Margaret wasn't offended by the personal question. She knew Catherine well enough to understand the question was prompted by genuine concern. She shrugged. "I've had some bad times, but for the most part, I'm doing fine."

Catherine nodded. "Good. And I hear your business is doing well, too."

"I hope so."

During their exchange, a small group of people had gathered around Mr. Sexy Eyes, and one of them—a pretty dark-haired young woman—said, "Oh, come on, Caleb!"

Caleb. Margaret liked the name. It was a strong name. It suited him.

The man named Caleb laughed. "Hey, come on. Give me a break. I'm not in the mood to do limericks right now."

Catherine chuckled, giving Margaret a sidelong glance. "Stick around. This should be good," she said.

"Who is he?" Margaret asked as nonchalantly as she could.

"Him? Oh, that's Caleb Mahoney. He's a prof in the English Department."

"Come on, Caleb, *pleeease,*" said the dark-haired young woman.

"Yeah, Caleb, come on. Be a sport," called a chubby man with a florid face.

"Maybe later."

Catherine said, "We do this at every party. People throw out women's names, and Caleb makes up limericks about them. He's good at it. No one's stumped him yet, no matter what name they give him."

Margaret would have liked to stay and watch, but she wasn't being paid to stand around like a guest. She excused herself and walked back to the kitchen. As she worked, she wondered if Caleb Mahoney had stuck to his guns or if he'd succumbed to the requests to do limericks. She could hear a lot of laughing from the other room.

Awhile later, as Margaret helped the servers remove the dirty dishes lying around, she looked for Caleb Mahoney. At first she didn't see him and thought he'd gone outside. Then, a few moments later, she spied him sitting on the love seat at the far end of the living room. Seated next to him was a garrulous old man Margaret had noticed earlier. Someone had remarked that the older gentleman was a retired professor, and Margaret had gathered that he was a real bore. The old man was gesticulating and talking, and Caleb sat quietly listening and nodding every once in awhile.

He didn't look at all bored, Margaret marveled. She wondered if Caleb Mahoney was just being nice or if he was really interested in what the old professor had to say. Then she wondered why she couldn't seem to stop thinking about Caleb Mahoney.

Twenty minutes later, Caleb still sat on the same love seat. Margaret, trying not to be obvious, worked her way around the crowd toward that part of the room. As she got closer, she overheard part of the conversation.

"I don't understand these young people today, Caleb," the old professor was saying. "They just don't want to work hard. There's no appreciation for the classics. It's MTV and movies and videos. They think if you can't say it in a dozen words or less, it doesn't need to be said.''

"You're right, Professor Kiddon," Caleb said. "I've noticed the same thing myself."

"They have the attention span of a gnat. Why, when you mention Lord Byron, they think you're talking about some kind of rock star!"

Margaret muffled a smile as she walked away. Actually the old professor was kind of funny. Still, it was nice of Caleb to sit there so long. She doubted if anyone else would have had that kind of patience.

The next time Margaret entered the living room, Caleb was no longer seated on the love seat. She looked slowly around the room, but he wasn't inside. Not many people were. From outside the open doors she heard someone tuning a fiddle. A few seconds later, the fiddle player launched into "The Orange Blossom Special."

Margaret wasn't musically inclined, but she recognized talent when she heard it, and the fiddle player was exceptional. The notes came pure, fast and hot. She wandered toward the French doors and peered outside.

Caleb Mahoney, surrounded by about forty of the guests, sat on a low bench at one end of the patio. The lively fiddle playing she'd heard emanated from his fingers and bow. Margaret watched, mesmerized, as Caleb played the intricate song with the sureness of a professional. She wondered where he'd learned to play like that.

When he finished with an extravagant sweep of the bow across the strings, he looked up, straight into her eyes. The people around him clapped, and Margaret, after a moment, clapped, too. She smiled, and he smiled back. Something warm and sweet swirled in her stomach, and for just a second, she felt like a young girl again.

"How about playing 'When Irish Eyes Are Smiling'?" someone asked.

Caleb chuckled. "Don't you ever get tired of the same old songs?" But his complaint was obviously good-natured, because he lifted the fiddle and began to play. Soon, several people began to sing, and then more joined in.

Once again, Margaret wished she could just stand there and watch, but she needed to get back to the kitchen. By the time she'd finished supervising the cleanup of the first round of food and had helped put out the desserts and coffee, the fiddle-playing session was over, and most of the guests were back inside. A tall brunette told a joke, and then someone else told another. As Margaret worked, she half listened. Just as she was about to return to the kitchen, someone said, "Okay, Caleb, *now* will you do the limericks?"

Margaret stopped. She couldn't help herself. She turned around. The pretty dark-haired young woman she'd noticed earlier stood next to Caleb.

He smiled down at her. "Okay," he said. "Give me a name." He sat on the arm of the couch.

"Jude," someone threw out.

"Let me see . . . Jude. Jude." He thought for a minute. "Okay. I've got it." Grinning, he chanted in a singsong voice, "I once knew a woman named Jude. Jude was a bit of a prude."

Margaret smiled.

Someone hooted. "Too easy. Jude was too easy."

"Shh, let him finish," someone else said.

Caleb continued, "Until one fine day, in the middle of May, when she suddenly got in the mood." His eyes twinkled.

"See? What did I tell you? Way too easy."

"I've got one," called a skinny man standing in the entrance to the dining room. "Nancy."

"Hmm," Caleb said. He thought for a while, then said, "I once met a woman named Nancy, to whom I took a great fancy. She started to pet me, and said she would let me, but only if I wasn't too antsy!"

"You can't stump Caleb," said the dark-haired woman. She smiled proudly.

"I'll stump him!" someone yelled triumphantly. "Sigourney. I'll bet you can't come up with a limerick for Sigourney!"

Everyone laughed and yelled. "Now we've got ya!"

Caleb Mahoney's blue eyes glowed with amusement and within seconds, he began, "I once knew a gal named Sigourney, who liked to wear jeans with a tore knee."

Everyone booed.

Margaret grinned.

Caleb raised his voice over the catcalls. "When I tried to bed her, she demanded I wed her..." He smiled in triumph.

Margaret thought he had the most charming smile she'd ever seen.

"And *voilà!* I was no longer *horny!*"

The guests howled. Margaret couldn't help laughing along with them, even though she'd never gone in for ribald humor of any kind. Somehow, out of the mouth of Caleb Mahoney, the word "horny" didn't sound ribald at all. It sounded...*sexy*. Just as the thought crossed her mind, Caleb's gaze turned in her direction, and their eyes met.

Margaret forgot to breathe. Her gaze was captured by those bottomless blue eyes, by the frank interest and admiration she saw there. Her heart beat faster, and for a moment, she felt so unsettled she couldn't look away.

Finally she did.

But for the rest of the evening, she kept thinking about Caleb Mahoney and how he had looked at her. She knew the memory of that look would remain with her for a long, long time.

And for the first time in years, Margaret suddenly wished she were younger.

Chapter Two

Caleb wondered what Margaret Desmond would say if he simply walked over to her, leaned down and whispered in her ear, "All night I've been thinking about how much I'd like to make love to you."

The thought made him smile. He knew if he were to act on his impulse, she'd blush furiously. He'd already seen her blush several times, and all he'd done to cause that reaction was look at her.

He wondered if she had any idea how beautiful she was. He had a feeling she didn't even think of herself in that way. A woman who knew she was beautiful walked in a certain way, held her head in a certain way and looked at a man in a certain way.

Margaret Desmond did none of those things. Margaret Desmond walked and acted like a woman who had never fully realized her potential.

She was a pleasure to watch. She reminded him of that English actress, Emma somebody. Margaret Desmond had that same patrician appearance—a clean, classy look that was timeless.

Caleb decided he liked everything about her, even the fact that she was more mature than most of the women he'd dated over the years. He was ready for someone calm and quiet, as Margaret seemed to be. Someone who wouldn't expect constant entertainment, who would appreciate the simple pleasures in life. He could easily imagine taking long walks with this woman, talking for hours about anything and everything.

His gaze followed her as she headed toward the kitchen, her arms full of serving plates. Her chin-length golden-brown hair, almost the exact shade of her eyes, bounced from her purposeful step.

Nice legs, he thought—and not for the first time. Some men were turned on by ample cleavage, but Caleb had always been a leg man. And Margaret Desmond certainly had legs worth looking at: long and slender, lightly tanned, with well-defined calf muscles and high arches. Yes, indeed, *very* nice legs.

He wondered if she'd started dating yet. After realizing she was at the party, it hadn't taken him more than an hour to find out her name and the fact that she was a recent widow. He wondered how she felt about younger men. Not that he was that much younger than she was. He figured she was probably in her early forties, which would make her only about four or five years older than he was, since he would be thirty-eight next month.

Four or five years wasn't much.

"She's very attractive, isn't she?" said a familiar voice behind him.

Caleb turned around, smiling as he recognized Catherine Higgins, one of his favorite colleagues. "Yes, she is. Do you know her?"

"As a matter of fact, I do."

Caleb waited. As he'd hoped, after a moment, Catherine continued.

"Margaret and I went to high school together."

Something, some hesitancy and reservation in Catherine's tone warned Caleb to be careful what he said and how he said it. "She's done a great job with the party."

Catherine nodded, giving him a measured look.

"Someone mentioned she's a recent widow." Caleb kept his voice casual, as if the comment was just an observation, nothing more.

"Yes. Her husband died of a heart attack back in January."

"That's too bad. He couldn't have been very old."

"No, he was just forty-nine."

"Did you know him, too?"

"Not well. He and Margaret socialized with a different circle of people." She hesitated, her blue eyes thoughtful. "I didn't much care for Anthony, but Margaret... well, I've always liked her enormously. She's a very nice woman."

Caleb would have liked to question Catherine further, but he figured it might be better not to be *too* curious about Margaret Desmond. He couldn't shake the feeling that Catherine wouldn't approve of his interest. Besides, he could find out anything else he wanted to know about the lovely Mrs. Desmond on his own.

He and Catherine talked about school for a while, then Catherine wandered off, and Caleb looked around for Margaret. For the rest of the evening, as he talked and mingled with the other guests, he kept one eye on her. About eleven-thirty, some of the guests began to leave, and Margaret, after clearing off the last of the food and dishes, disappeared into the kitchen.

Caleb strolled over to where Dean Anderson and his wife stood saying goodbye to departing guests. Caleb joined the group, and ten minutes later he walked out into the warm summer night with several other guests.

"G'night, Caleb," they said as they headed toward their cars, parked up and down the street.

"'Night." Caleb headed for the back of the house, where he stood in the shadows off to one side of the driveway. Parked near the back door was a large blue van with the words Party Line stenciled on the side. He figured it must belong to Margaret.

He lit a cigarette—only his second of the evening since he was trying to quit—and quietly smoked. Through the kitchen windows, he saw Margaret moving back and forth inside. He waited patiently, knowing that soon the catering crew would finish their cleanup and Margaret would leave. The night noises settled around him: a chorus of crickets, the croak of a frog from the pond that backed up to the Anderson property, the muted sounds of the cleanup going on inside the house.

Caleb finished his cigarette and ground it out beneath his foot. His patience was rewarded about twelve-thirty. The back door opened, and Margaret stood silhouetted in the doorway. So as not to startle her, Caleb walked toward her as soon as she stepped onto the back porch. Even so, she jumped slightly when he moved into view.

"Oh," she said. "I—I didn't know anyone was out here."

He smiled. "I tried not to scare you."

"You didn't. Not really." She looked at him curiously.

"I've been waiting for you."

She stared at him. "Waiting for me?"

He nodded. "I thought you might need some help carrying everything out and loading it in your van." He walked closer and reached for the large carton she held in her arms. "That *is* your van, isn't it?" He began to walk toward the vehicle. "By the way, I'm Caleb Mahoney."

"Yes, I—I know. Someone mentioned your name when you were doing the limericks." Her voice was soft and low, as he'd known it would be.

By now they'd reached the van, and she unlocked the back doors. He placed the carton inside, then turned to face her. Her face was bathed with moonlight, and there was something fragile and vulnerable about her as she looked up at him. He had an almost irresistible urge to put his arms around her and pull her close.

"Thank you," she said. Then awkwardly, she stuck out her hand. "I'm Margaret Desmond."

"Hello, Margaret Desmond." Caleb took her hand. It felt smooth and warm and surprisingly strong as it slid into his. For several heartbeats, they stood there, hands joined, looking at each other, neither saying anything. As the navy night folded around them, Caleb was filled with a strange sense of destiny, as if all of his life he'd been moving toward this moment.

Then the Andersons' back door opened, and one of Margaret's helpers walked out, and the spell was broken. Margaret withdrew her hand and turned away from him. Caleb followed her back to the house, and along with the two helpers, they loaded all of her supplies into the van. Once the other two women had gotten into their cars and gone, Margaret said, "Well, Professor Mahoney, thank you. It was very considerate of you to stay behind and help us."

"Please. My name is Caleb. Only my students call me Professor Mahoney."

She nodded.

"And my motive in staying behind wasn't entirely altruistic."

"Oh?" The back porch light illuminated her face as she met his gaze.

She had the most beautiful eyes, he decided. Guileless, trusting, completely honest. They were the kind of eyes a man could get happily lost in. "No, I have to admit, I simply wanted a chance to talk with you...alone."

She swallowed, and Caleb's gaze followed the movement. A little pulse beat at the base of her throat, and he wished he could touch it. Her mouth opened slightly, but she said nothing.

He really liked that about her. That she could remain quiet and not feel the necessity to fill the silence. He knew she was waiting for him to explain.

"From the first moment I saw you—the other day at registration—I wanted to meet you," he began.

She tilted her head to the side in a quizzical gesture, a little half smile playing around her lips, but she still said nothing.

"You intrigued me. You still do."

"Professor Ma—"

"Caleb."

"Caleb." She sighed. "I'm flattered, but—"

"Please...Margaret...hear me out. Okay?"

She sighed again, and those eyes studied him. Then she nodded. "All right."

"I was hoping we could get to know each other."

"I don't think—"

"You promised to hear me out."

Now she smiled, and amusement fired her topaz eyes.

"I was hoping you'd have dinner with me tomorrow night."

She shook her head.

"Lunch tomorrow afternoon, then."

She continued shaking her head. "No, I'm sorry, I can't."

"Why not?"

"It's just not a good idea."

"But why not?"

"Well, for one thing, I'm a recent widow."

"I know that."

She shrugged. "Well, then you should understand."

"Catherine Higgins told me it's been eight months since your husband died."

She seemed startled by his statement and didn't answer for a minute. "Look, as I started to say before, I'm flattered by your offer, but I just can't."

Caleb thought it was revealing that she hadn't answered his statement directly. "I still don't understand why not."

She shrugged. "I told you. It's not a good idea."

"But why do you say that? You're single. I'm single. And we're attracted to each other. We *are* attracted to each other, aren't we?"

She couldn't quite meet his eyes, and he knew, just from the way her breathing had quickened, that his question had flustered her. He also knew she couldn't deny what he'd said, because if she did, she would be lying. And she knew he would know it. "Well, aren't we?" he persisted.

Now she looked up, and those wonderful eyes met his squarely. Her amusement had faded. "Whether we are or not isn't important. The answer is still no." She shut the doors to the van, then said, "Thanks again. It's late, and I've got to get going."

He helped her into the van. She fastened her seat belt, then shut the door and rolled down the window.

He said, "You know, Margaret Desmond, I don't give up easily."

She smiled, started the engine, then waved as she carefully backed out of the driveway.

Caleb waited until he could no longer see the red taillights of her van before starting the short walk home.

All the way home Margaret relived the delicious feelings Caleb Mahoney had aroused in her. She'd so wanted to say yes to him. So wanted to go out with him. But how could she? Not only was it too soon for her to date—after all, Anthony had only been dead eight months—and Margaret could just imagine what her mother and children would think if she were to begin dating already, but Caleb Mahoney? The young professor, as appealing and charming as he was, was entirely unsuitable.

He was far too young, for one thing. Why, he must be seven or eight years younger than she was. Perhaps more. My God, her mother would have a conniption. Joyce Guthrie had spent her entire life doing the proper thing, and she'd raised both Margaret and Margaret's younger sister, Madelyn, to behave the same way. And so far, the only time Margaret had ever disappointed her mother was when she'd married Anthony at so young an age.

Margaret smiled ruefully. Joyce had never let her forget that transgression, either. Margaret had spent the past twenty-seven years striving to make it up to her mother by being the most perfect wife and mother and respectful daughter and daughter-in-law she could be.

She'd succeeded, too. Her place in Riverview, her place in life, was solidly entrenched. Satisfyingly entrenched, she told herself. She was content. Her vague feelings of dissatisfaction were perfectly normal, and they would pass. Although she'd never expected to become a widow at so young an age, she really had everything she'd ever wanted: a lovely home, equally lovely children—for surely Lori would eventually grow up—and now a promising business.

And soon she would be a grandmother. Margaret smiled again, but this time with happiness. Lisa, her oldest child, was expecting her first baby in December, and Margaret was almost as excited about the event as Lisa and her husband, Keith.

Remembering the imminent arrival of her first grandchild only emphasized how foolhardy any type of involvement with the young professor would be. No, Caleb Mahoney had no place in Margaret's life.

But she had to admit, she *was* flattered that he'd seemed so interested. Who wouldn't be flattered? Caleb Mahoney was the sexiest man she'd ever seen. That combination of dark hair, blue eyes and boyish charm was potent. Lethal, even.

Margaret shivered. The way he had looked at her tonight had made her feel so incredibly feminine. No one, including Anthony, *especially Anthony,* had ever made her feel quite that way before. As if . . . as if . . .

She shivered again. She'd felt all tingly when Caleb had looked at her, as if his hands were touching her instead of his eyes. She swallowed. She'd felt as if he were making love to her.

Slow, erotic love.

Margaret braked for a red light and shook her head at her foolishness. What did she know of slow, erotic lovemaking? Anthony had been her first, last and only lover, and when Anthony had made love to her, it had been fast and matter-of-fact. That's all she'd ever known. Anything else had strictly been her imagination, ideas garnered from books and movies and songs.

She sighed, remembering a song that had once been popular about a lover with slow hands. The lyrics had always caused her to feel an ache inside because she'd known she was missing something, yet felt powerless to do anything about it. If she'd dared to suggest anything different to Anthony, he would have taken her suggestions as criticism, and Anthony had not tolerated criticism well. Especially any that would have cast aspersions on his manliness.

So all Margaret could do was dream. And pretend. And wonder. Eventually she had become reconciled to the knowledge that she would never know about slow-handed lovers or anything else remotely connected.

Until now.

Until tonight.

Until Caleb Mahoney had held her hand in his, and she'd felt the warm blood coursing through his veins, seen the interest smoldering in his deep blue eyes, heard the promise resonant in the rich fullness of his voice.

Margaret sighed again as she turned into her subdivision. Forget him, she told herself with regret.

Caleb Mahoney is not for you.

Margaret groaned and rolled over. A noise that didn't belong—a loud noise—had intruded on her wonderful dream. She pulled her pillow over her head and tried to lose herself once more.

But now another noise penetrated her makeshift shield.

The doorbell.

Her doorbell.

Margaret, suddenly fully awake, sat up in bed. She knuckled her eyes, then glanced at the bedside clock. Seven-thirty. Good grief, who could possibly be calling on her at seven-thirty in the morning?

Margaret swung her feet out of bed, and reached for her peach cotton robe. She drew it on, tied the belt and walked barefoot out of her bedroom, down the hall, and down the staircase.

About midway, she heard the revving of an engine, then the same loud noise that had first awakened her. It sounded like a motorcycle roaring off down the street.

A motorcycle?

No one on her street, and certainly no one she knew, owned a motorcycle. She hurried to the bottom of the stairs.

The morning sun, already strong, poured through the stained-glass panels on either side of the double walnut front door as Margaret reached for the dead bolt. She unlocked the door, then opened it.

Her mouth dropped open.

Sitting on her front stoop, right next to her morning paper, was an enormous wicker picnic basket. Protruding from the half-opened top was the neck of a wine bottle, and tied to the handle with a white satin ribbon was a single red rosebud wrapped in tissue.

"What in the world?" She reached down to lift the basket. Taped to the top was a small, square white envelope.

Mystified, Margaret removed the envelope and opened it. She withdrew the single sheet of paper and read it.

Dear Margaret,
   If you've changed your mind about having lunch with me, I'll be waiting for you by the gazebo at the river at one o'clock this afternoon.

                                                          Caleb

Still holding the note, Margaret looked up. Her dazed eyes looked slowly up and down the street. There was no one in sight.

She picked up the paper and carried it and the basket inside. When she reached the kitchen, she placed the basket and paper on the table. She removed the rose from the handle and opened the wicker container.

Inside were a cold roasted chicken wrapped in foil, a loaf of French bread, a wheel of Brie, two sweet red peppers, a cluster of green grapes, the bottle of wine—a German reisling—and a bag of potato chips.

"Potato chips?" she said, laughing.

The last thing she removed from the basket was a crystal bud vase. Astonished, she recognized it as Waterford.

How in the world had he managed this? she wondered. Did he just happen to have all of these things on hand? It had only been a little over seven hours since she'd last seen Caleb.

Thoroughly bemused, she sank onto a kitchen chair. She stared at the contents of the basket, thought about the note. This behavior of Caleb's was completely foreign to anything she'd ever known.

Anthony had not been spontaneous or imaginative. She couldn't imagine him ever doing anything like this, even when they'd first met. The most romantic and spontaneous thing Anthony had ever done was send her roses on Valentine's Day. And even then, he'd only done it once or twice.

No, Caleb Mahoney was the exact opposite of Anthony, in almost every way. Certainly he didn't look anything like Anthony. Her late husband had been heavily built. A big, tall man with blond hair and light gray eyes. He'd been a man's man. Bluff and hearty. He had played football and golf. He had enjoyed thick steaks and hard liquor. There was nothing subtle about him.

Someone like Caleb, who wore his hair too long, who played the fiddle and made up limericks, was the kind of person Anthony would have made fun of.

Margaret grinned. Maybe that was recommendation enough for her to take Caleb up on his offer. After all, Margaret couldn't stand most of the people Anthony had admired.

Now just a minute. You're long past the rebellious stage. And Anthony is gone. You don't have to prove anything to anyone.

Rising slowly, Margaret took the chicken, the cheese and the wine and placed them in the refrigerator. She would have to return them to Caleb, she decided, ignoring the twinge of regret she felt. Later today, in the afternoon, she would look in the telephone book and see if he was listed, then she would drive over to his house and leave the basket on his doorstep.

That decided, she turned on the coffeemaker, and after showering and dressing for the day, she fixed herself a cup of coffee and opened the morning paper.

She tried to read the news, but out of the corner of her eye, she kept seeing the picnic basket, and thoughts of Caleb and his note and his eyes kept ruining her concentration.

"Darn you!" she finally said, throwing down the paper. She got up and walked to the sink where she rinsed out her coffee cup. She closed her eyes. "Darn you, Caleb Mahoney," she whispered. "I was perfectly happy with my life. I was just beginning to get things together, and now you've come along to spoil everything!" She felt absurdly close to tears, which made her even madder. She reached into the pocket of her shorts for a tissue and blew her nose. You're being ridiculous, she told herself. A little flirting and attention, and you've gone all to pieces.

The doorbell chimed, and she whirled around. Her heart gave a giant leap. Caleb! Had he come back? She swallowed hard, and headed for the front door. She wished she'd put on some makeup. She looked down at her beige shorts and plain white blouse. Her bare feet. Well, maybe it was just as well she looked so plain. Now Caleb would see her for what she really was—a middle-aged, soon-to-be-grandmother—and he would surely decide he'd made a monumental mistake.

Margaret wasn't sure if she was relieved or disappointed when she opened the door to find her best friend, Rosemary Beil, standing there, looking striking in a hot pink dress with matching hat.

"Rosemary! Come on in." Pleasure warmed her voice. "What're you doing here? Shouldn't you be at work?"

"Oh, I had to pay a call on old Mr. Gossett. He was giving Sam a lot of grief and threatening not to renew his ad."

The Sam Rosemary had referred to was one of her advertising sales people, Margaret knew, and Mr. Gossett was the president of the First National Bank of Riverview. For the past two years, First National had had a contract for a half-page ad in the business section of the Sunday edition of the *Riverview Record*. Rosemary had once explained to Margaret that the backbone of the paper was its contract advertisers.

"I'm glad you stopped. Come on in," Margaret said. The two walked back to the big kitchen.

"Want some coffee?" Margaret offered as Rosemary removed her hat and sat at the table.

"Is the Pope Catholic?"

Margaret chuckled, poured the coffee, then joined her friend. "Is the hat new?" She picked up the wide-brimmed white straw trimmed in hot pink cabbage roses.

Rosemary grinned. "Uh-huh. You know me. I saw it at Heather's Hattery and couldn't resist it."

Hats were Rosemary's trademark. She wore them everywhere, winter and summer, and had probably long ago lost count of the number she owned. "I swear, Ro, you keep Heather's going single-handedly."

Rosemary grinned. "We all need *some* vices. Except you, of course," she added, her dark eyes twinkling.

Margaret looked at her friend with affection. Rosemary, with her black curly hair, dark eyes and olive skin, was dramatic and striking, if not classically pretty. "Oh, I have my vices," Margaret said.

"I wish you'd tell me what they are. Then maybe I wouldn't feel so intimidated by you."

Margaret laughed. "Intimidated? That'll be the day. Nothing intimidates you, and you know it." Margaret couldn't remember how many times she'd wished she had half of Rosemary's self-confidence and assurance. Rosemary did everything well. The only thing Margaret had ever done well was be a mother and wife.

"I didn't come here to talk about me," Rosemary said. "Tell me about last night's party. How'd it go?"

"It went really well, I think. Everyone seemed to like the food, and there were no hitches at all." Unless, of course, a person considered Caleb Mahoney a hitch.

"I knew it would." Rosemary sipped her coffee and glanced around idly. "You going on a picnic?" She was looking at the picnic basket, which Margaret had moved to the counter.

"Oh, no, I . . . uh . . ." She stopped in confusion.

Rosemary grinned. "Hey, Magpie, it's a simple question. All you have to do is answer, yes, I'm going on a picnic, or no, I'm not going."

Margaret laughed self-consciously. "Well, no, I'm not going on a picnic."

"Then why, pray tell, do you have a picnic basket sitting out?" Rosemary's dark eyes were alight with curiosity, the same way they looked when she was on the trail of a good story.

Margaret met her friend's gaze. "It's a long story."

"I'm not in any hurry."

Margaret only hesitated a moment. She wanted to tell someone about Caleb, and she trusted Rosemary more than anyone else in the world. So she told her about seeing him at registration. And about seeing him at the party. She told Rosemary everything, even how he'd made her feel when he'd taken her hand.

"Caleb Mahoney, huh? My, my, my," Rosemary said as her friend finished.

"You know him?"

Rosemary chuckled. "Of course, I know him. I know everybody who's anybody in this town."

Margaret should have guessed. Rosemary really *did* know everyone. That was one of the reasons she'd made a success of the newspaper. "What do you think of him?" she asked quietly.

"You mean aside from the fact that he's a hunk?"

Margaret smiled. "Yes, aside from that."

"Actually, from what I know of him, he's a pretty decent guy. A little on the hard-to-pin-down side. Kind of a free-spirit renaissance man." She gave Margaret a thoughtful gaze. "The kind of guy it'd be great to have a fling with. Not the kind of guy for picket fences and wedding rings."

"I'm not looking for picket fences and wedding rings."

"You sure?"

"I'm very sure. I've been married once. That was enough." When Rosemary gave her a quizzical look, Margaret added, "Over the past months, I've discovered I like making my own decisions and running my own life." Margaret felt guilty giving voice to her thoughts, but doggedly continued. "It . . . it's very nice not to have to worry about someone else's feelings and desires before I do anything."

Rosemary grinned. "Good for you, my friend. That's a real healthy attitude."

"You don't think it's selfish?"

"Hell, no," Rosemary said. "I think it's honest and normal. Most women, if given the chance, would feel the exact same way—even the ones who profess to be blissfully married."

Margaret smiled. She could always count on Rosemary's support.

"But all that aside," Rosemary said, "you're still thinking about going to the river this afternoon, aren't you?"

"No, I'm not."

But she was.

She was, and Rosemary knew it. You could see the knowledge in the depths of her eyes. Margaret could also see the concern.

"Listen, Magpie, be careful. You could get hurt."

"I thought you said Caleb Mahoney was a decent guy."

"He is. He's a sweetie, in fact, but he's also the kind of guy who can break your heart. Caleb, well, he believes in living life to the fullest. Taking his pleasure where he finds it. A woman like you isn't made for a roll in the hay and then a quick goodbye, it's been great kind of thing. You care too much. You give too much of yourself to any relationship."

"Don't worry, Ro, I'm not going to meet him. Although if getting burned were my only consideration, I might take the chance. But Caleb's too young, and it's too soon. My entire family would be scandalized, and I'm just not up to it."

"He's not too young, and it's not too soon, either."

"I thought you didn't want me to go."

"I don't, but those aren't the reasons why. You. Your feelings. That's what I care about."

Love surged through Margaret. What would she do without Rosemary? Anytime she had ever felt down or inadequate or unhappy, Rosemary had always been there to prop her up.

"You're a wonderful friend, you know that?" she said. "But I'm not going to get involved with Caleb Mahoney, so you can quit worrying."

Chapter Three

After Rosemary left, Margaret busied herself around the house. She tried to ignore the clock. What did it matter that the time was creeping toward eleven?

About eleven-thirty, she settled herself at her desk in the upstairs sitting room. She would go over the business accounts and pay some bills.

Unfortunately the little ormolu clock gracing the right corner of her cherrywood desk kept catching her attention. Its ticking seemed relentlessly loud.

Margaret tapped her cloisonné pen against her ledger. *Quit looking at the clock!* Resolutely she looked down at the figures she'd been adding.

Tick, tick, tick.

Margaret threw down her pen and glared at the clock. *I am not going.* She kept saying the words in her head, again and again, as if by saying them enough times she would convince herself of their validity.

She chewed on her lower lip. She wished she could stop thinking about Caleb's note, about how he would feel when he waited at the gazebo and she never showed up.

Would he be disappointed? Angry?

Oh, quit flattering yourself. He'll probably just shrug his shoulders and forget about you. Just because he made you feel as if you were special to him doesn't mean you really are. Maybe he showers this kind of attention on all the women he meets.

She tore her gaze from the clock's face and stared at the ornate white-and-gold desk phone sitting to her left. Regardless of Caleb's motives in asking her out today, the fact remained that he had. A considerate person would call him and let him know she wasn't coming.

She was still thinking about calling him when the phone rang. She snatched up the receiver, grateful for the distraction. "Hello?"

"Mom?"

"Oh...hi, Lisa!" Margaret forced her thoughts away from Caleb and smiled. She genuinely enjoyed talking to her oldest child. Lisa, at twenty-six, was everything any mother could want in a daughter. She possessed a sweet disposition, was loving and attentive toward Margaret—especially since Anthony's death—and was a happy young wife expecting her first child. She had fulfilled all Margaret's hopes and expectations. "What are you and Keith up to this morning?" Margaret asked.

"Keith is painting the baby's room, and I just finished baking a cake for the picnic."

Margaret had forgotten that this afternoon was Keith's company's picnic. *No wonder. You've been too busy thinking about another kind of picnic, haven't you?*

"What've you been doing this morning?" Lisa asked.

"Oh, nothing much. Paying some bills. And Rosemary stopped by earlier."

"How did the party go last night?"

"Wonderful." Margaret filled Lisa in on the details of the previous evening.

"So what're your plans for the rest of the day?" Lisa asked when her mother had finished.

Margaret looked at the clock. "I don't know. I have dozens of things I *could* do, but I haven't decided yet." A picture of Caleb standing by the gazebo flashed through her mind.

They talked for a little while longer, then Lisa said, "I want you to come to dinner tomorrow night. I bought some steaks, and Keith's going to do them on the grill. His parents are coming, too."

Dolly and Floyd Hubbard, Lisa's in-laws, were not high on the list of Margaret's favorite people. Dolly was a whiner, and Floyd too self-righteous and bigoted for Margaret's taste, but she ignored the negative thoughts Lisa's mention of her in-laws had conjured and forced enthusiasm into her voice. "Thanks, honey. I'd love to come. What time?"

"About five. We'll eat early, okay?"

"Sounds lovely."

"Well, I'd better be going," Lisa said. "We're supposed to leave by one, and I haven't showered yet."

"Bye, honey," Margaret said. "Have a good time today."

"You, too."

You, too.

Margaret grimaced. *You, too.* Yesterday, before the party, she had been looking forward to today—her first free Saturday in weeks. Now, though, she couldn't banish a restless feeling.

She eyed the clock again: 11:53. Her gaze turned to the opened ledger. She stared at the unadded column and the unpaid bills, then slowly closed the book. Like a magnet, the clock pulled her gaze back to its small face.

11:54.

In exactly sixty-six minutes, Caleb Mahoney would be waiting at the gazebo.

Let him wait. I am not going.

Margaret stood. She walked out of the sitting room and down the hall to her bedroom, heading straight for the dormer window. Slowly she parted the sheer white curtains and stared down at her sleepy suburban street—at the big homes and manicured yards and expensive cars.

She swallowed. She could feel her heart beating. As if she were someone in a dream, she turned, her gaze fastening on her bedside clock radio. The digital numbers glowed.

11:59.

As she watched, they changed.

12:00.

Suddenly, as if her hands and body were working independently of her brain, Margaret began to strip off her clothes.

Forty-five minutes later, dressed in dark green shorts and her new yellow blouse, the repacked picnic basket on the seat beside her, Margaret backed out of the driveway and pointed her car toward the river.

* * *

Caleb hadn't felt this nervous since he was a junior in high school when he'd invited Brigitte Costello to the prom. He had dressed carefully before coming to the river, in his favorite stone-washed jeans and a dark blue T-shirt that someone had once told him matched his eyes.

He'd splashed cologne on and carefully combed his hair. Then he grinned at his reflection in his bathroom mirror. He wondered if Margaret would even show up, let alone notice the trouble he'd gone to to impress her.

He couldn't figure out why today was so important to him. Either she'd come, or she wouldn't. It wasn't a big deal. Win some, lose some, he told himself.

Yet today *was* important to him. There was something special about Margaret Desmond. Something very special. He simply couldn't accept that she wouldn't come.

But now, as he stood with his back to the gazebo and looked down the sloping bank toward the Tomhannock River, he knew he would have no choice but to accept her decision if she didn't show up. He had never forced himself on a woman, and he had no intention of starting now.

He glanced at his utilitarian watch. Five minutes to one. His gaze swept the area, dotted here and there with people enjoying the last summer weekend before the start of the school year and the onset of autumn.

He looked up, toward the parking area, and just as he did, a big gray Cadillac pulled into view. Even before she stepped out, Caleb knew the car belonged to Margaret.

He smiled.

* * *

What am I doing here? Margaret asked herself as she climbed out of the Cadillac. Her stomach felt queasy, as if she were ill, but she knew her reaction was caused by nerves, not illness.

Then she saw Caleb. The strong August sun glinted off his shiny dark hair as he climbed the hill toward her.

Her pulse quickened as he came nearer, her impressions all jumbled. She noted the form-fitting jeans, the equally form-fitting blue T-shirt, his tanned arms and face. As he came closer, she saw the warmth and pleasure in his eyes, which today, in the sunlight, looked as deep and blue as the river below.

Seeing him, feeling the strength of her attraction to him hit her with a fresh onslaught of emotions, Margaret was glad she had worn sunglasses. She wasn't sure she wanted Caleb to know how he made her feel. She was absolutely sure she didn't want him to know how uncertain, how downright scared, she felt, and she knew her eyes always gave away her feelings.

What was she doing here? she thought again, panic threatening to overwhelm her. Was she nuts? Her peripheral vision told her there were dozens of people in the park and all along the river. By this evening, half of Riverview would know that Margaret Desmond, the forty-five-year-old widow of Anthony Desmond, had been here and met Caleb Mahoney, the sexy, thirty-something professor from the college.

By tomorrow morning, the other half would know. And by tomorrow afternoon, no later, Margaret's mother would be calling her, asking her if she'd lost her mind. And what could Margaret answer but yes?

"You came," Caleb said as he reached the parking lot. He stopped a couple of feet away. His smile faded as their eyes met.

She nodded, incapable of speech.

"I'm very glad." The words were soft and washed over her like gentle spring rain. She couldn't have answered him if her life had depended upon it. Then, surprising her, he reached over and removed her sunglasses. His fingers brushed her cheek, and Margaret trembled. "There," he said, smiling again. "That's a whole lot better. Now I can see your eyes. You have incredibly beautiful eyes."

Something in the vicinity of Margaret's heart squeezed painfully. She wanted to look away, but she couldn't. Something more potent than her puny fears was at work here, and at that moment she felt powerless to oppose it.

"Did you bring the food?" he asked, still smiling down at her.

"Yes, I, uh, it's right there on the front seat." She gestured toward the car.

"I'll get it." Caleb opened the door and took out the basket. His smile mesmerized her. "Ready?"

Margaret wet her lips. "Just let me lock the car first." Turning her back on him, she used the time it took her to insert her key into the lock and turn it to gather her wits and calm her turbulent emotions.

When she again faced Caleb, he reached for her hand. After only a moment's hesitation, Margaret slid her hand into his and tried not to think about how good it felt there, how right it felt there. Carrying the basket with his other hand, he said, "Come on. I've already picked out a place for our picnic."

He led her down the hill and to the left, where a trail began that wound through the wooded park paralleling the river. As they walked along, the river glistening on their right, Margaret's doubts assailed her again. She tried to think of something to say. She felt awkward and unsure of herself, feelings that she despised. She was sure Caleb would soon realize what a mistake he'd made in inviting her out with him. She knew all too well that she wasn't witty and clever, that she couldn't make scintillating conversation and had no talent for snappy banter.

Oh, God, why did I come? He'll be bored silly within one hour.

If she hadn't known how utterly stupid she'd look, she would have yanked her hand loose, turned around and run back to her car. Her misgivings nearly overwhelmed her as they walked deep into the park, into a thicket of pine trees a few hundred yards back from the river. "Here we are," Caleb said, letting go of her hand and pointing to a quilt lying on a bed of pine needles. In the middle of the quilt sat a paper bag.

She eyed the quilt, marveling at his foresight in bringing it. Her doubts grew stronger as she wondered how often he'd done this kind of thing. Maybe he had arranged dozens of such picnics, with dozens of women. Maybe all of this was part of a careful plan of seduction. Maybe the feeling that she was special was a delusion on her part—a delusion she had wanted to believe because it made her feel good. And maybe Caleb Mahoney had understood all of this. Because he'd certainly pushed all the right buttons to get her here, hadn't he? "What's in the bag?" she asked to fill the suddenly oppressive silence.

He grinned. "Plates and utensils. I forgot to put them in the basket."

"You've thought of everything." Unlike her. She had tried to keep from thinking at all as she'd hurried to get ready. Thinking might have made her change her mind. After all, this wasn't exactly a rational or sensible decision on her part.

"I try." He set the picnic basket down at the edge of the quilt, then, turning to her, he bowed low. "Madame. Please have a seat."

Feeling desperately awkward and self-conscious, as well as racked by uncertainty, Margaret gingerly sat on one side of the quilt. She drew her knees up to her chest and hugged them. Caleb dropped to his knees and began unloading the picnic basket. "Why don't you get the plates and stuff out?" he said.

Reluctantly Margaret abandoned the illusion of safety the barrier her knees had provided and reached for the paper bag. She extracted two large paper plates, a handful of napkins, two plastic wineglasses, and stainless-steel utensils.

When all the food was arranged, Caleb stretched out on the other side of the quilt and, propping his head up on his hand, looked at her. Approval and admiration radiated from his eyes as he said, "Did I tell you how glad I am you came today?"

Margaret could feel her face warming. Her stupid heart accelerated, too. "Yes." She met his gaze and instantly felt that same drowning sensation she'd experienced before. She wanted to look away, but she couldn't.

"I kept telling myself if you didn't come, it wasn't a big deal, but I knew I didn't mean it."

Margaret didn't know how to answer him. She was totally out of her depth here. She had lost the art of flirting, if she'd ever had it. She wasn't even sure Caleb was flirting with her. Perhaps this was simply the way men talked to women nowadays. She nervously wet her lips, and saw his gaze follow the path of her tongue.

Something coiled tightly deep inside her. Caleb's eyes slowly met hers again.

So blue, she thought. So sincere.

As they looked at each other, sounds of the summer day drifted around them: voices raised in shouts and laughter, birds chattering as they flitted through the trees, a car's backfire, the soft slap of oars from a distant canoe. The sun streamed through the tall pines, making shifting patterns of light and dark against Caleb's hair and skin. Behind him, in a clump between two trees, were late-blooming buttercups in shades of yellow and scarlet. Margaret was aware of all this, but only as a pale backdrop to the vivid emotions pulsating through her.

The snap of pine needles dragged Margaret out of her trancelike state as a teenage couple, arms wound around each other's waists, walked about a dozen yards away from their picnic site. She looked down at the food, then back up again.

"Are you hungry?" Caleb asked.

"A little." She wasn't, not really, but eating would give her something to do. Something other than drowning in his eyes.

She reached for the bread and broke off the end. She avoided his gaze as he handed her the cheese. She cut herself a wedge, and he uncorked the wine.

Soon they were eating. He ate with enthusiasm, the way she was sure he did everything. They didn't talk, for which Margaret was grateful. Although she hadn't been hungry, she managed to finish her bread and cheese, and even ate a small piece of chicken along with a slice of sweet red pepper. Caleb polished off three pieces of chicken, two big hunks of bread and then started on the grapes.

"Ahh, that was good," he said, patting his stomach.

"Yes, it was. Thank you." Lordy, couldn't she think of anything more interesting to say? He must be wishing he were anywhere but here, with anyone but her.

He poured himself another glass of wine and motioned toward hers, which was still half-full. Margaret, who didn't normally drink much, held out her glass. Perhaps it would help her relax to have a bit more wine. Perhaps it would help her think of something to say.

"Tell me about yourself," he said, stretching back out again.

Margaret looked at the shimmering river. "There's nothing much to tell." She twisted her wineglass in her hands. "I'm a widow with three grown children...." She hesitated. Oh, shoot, she might as well get it all out in the open. "And I have a grandchild on the way. A girl. Due in early December." She looked at him to see how he'd react to her news.

He smiled. "Grandmothers never looked like you when I was a kid." His eyes studied her as he took a swallow of wine. "I know it sounds clichéd, but you must have been a child bride."

Margaret nodded, pleased by his response even though she'd told herself she didn't care what he thought about her impending grandmotherhood. "I got married when I was eighteen."

"How old are you now?"

So they'd get everything out in the open today. Good. Then maybe he'd see how ridiculous this was and he wouldn't call her again. "I'm forty-five." She took another sip of her wine. She might as well go for broke. "How old are you?"

"Thirty-seven." He said it matter-of-factly, as if the difference in their ages didn't matter.

But those eight years loomed like a high wall in Margaret's mind. All she could think was that Caleb was only eleven years older than Lisa. He had been an eleven-year-old boy when her daughter was born. Suddenly the eight years' difference in their ages seemed insurmountable. What in God's name was she doing here? This was the craziest thing she'd ever done.

"So what are your kids like?" Caleb asked.

Margaret stared at him. Didn't he realize how insane this was? Wasn't he going to say anything about their ages? Her throat felt dry as she answered. "Lisa is twenty-six. She's my oldest and the one who's expecting the baby. She lives here in Riverview. Her husband is Keith Hubbard. You've probably heard of his father. Floyd Hubbard? The family has a big construction company." The words tumbled out, while all the while she kept thinking, eight years, eight years.

Something flickered in the depths of Caleb's eyes as he said, "Oh, yes, Floyd Hubbard. He's the driving force behind the airport consortium, isn't he?"

"Yes." The town of Riverview had been in the throes of a full-scale war over whether or not to allow the construction of an airport on lands that were currently serving as a bird refuge. Feelings ran high on both sides of the issue, and Margaret had listened to Floyd expound on the subject many times.

"What about your other kids?"

"After Lisa comes my son, Tony, who's twenty-four. He's a pharmacist, and he and his wife Darcy live in Glens Falls."

"Not too far away."

"No, not far at all."

"And your third child?"

"Lori. She's my youngest. She just turned eighteen a couple of months ago, and she's enrolled at Riverview College."

He smiled. "She is? Not an English major, is she?"

Margaret shook her head. "No, she's studying drama." She smiled ruefully. "She wants to be an actress."

"My sister's an actress."

"Really?"

"Uh-huh. She's got a part in a soap opera. 'Lovers and Liars.' Have you ever seen it?"

"Yes! I have," Margaret said, impressed. "What part does your sister play?"

"She plays Barbara, one of the twins."

Barbara and Beverly Henderson were the younger sisters of the main character on the popular soap. As Margaret pictured the actress who played Barbara, she realized the young woman bore a distinct resemblance to Caleb. She had the same dark hair, although hers was wildly curly, and the same intense blue eyes. "That's wonderful. You must really be proud of her."

"Yeah, I am."

"Do you have any other brothers and sisters?"

He grinned. "Afraid so. In fact, I'm one of seven. In addition to Sue—the one who's an actress—I have two other sisters and three brothers."

"Seven!"

He grimaced. "Awful, isn't it?"

"Not at all. In fact, I envy you. I always wanted to belong to a big family. I'll bet you're all so close." Margaret knew her voice sounded wistful.

Caleb shrugged. "Yeah, well, I guess we are. But being in a big family is not all it's cracked up to be."

"Tell me what it was like."

"Well, my dad was a cop, and cops in New York City—hell, cops everywhere—are notoriously underpaid. We lived in one half of a brownstone duplex in the Bronx, and we never seemed to have any money. I shared a bedroom with my three brothers until I was eighteen and started college."

Caleb swatted at a pesky fly, then sat up and reached for the now-empty paper bag. He and Margaret both stood and began to clean up the remains of their meal as he continued to talk. "When I think of my childhood," he said, "I always think of noise. My mother is a voice teacher, and because she couldn't afford a babysitter for us kids, she gave lessons in our house. There were always people around, always something going on. There wasn't ever a corner I could call my own."

"I still envy you." Margaret couldn't imagine growing up in the atmosphere he'd described. Her own existence had been so quiet, so circumscribed, and so boring. Her mother hadn't worked. Her father was a doctor before his retirement and subsequent death three years ago. Both Joyce and Charles Guthrie had always been socially correct, reserved people. They had never encouraged Margaret or her sister to have their friends around.

"Are you an only child?" he asked.

"No. I have one sister, but we're not very close." That was an understatement, Margaret thought, as a clear image of Madelyn's cool, judgmental eyes filled her head. Every time her younger sister looked at her, Margaret could feel her disdain as clearly as if Madelyn had spoken. Madelyn was bright, forceful and accomplished—a doctor like their father—and Margaret knew her sister found her sadly lacking.

He shrugged. "I guess we all wish for the opposite of what we have. I know I sure did." Something in his tone of voice made Margaret wonder if he had secret feelings, too. If one of his siblings had found him as lacking as Madelyn had found her. His eyes glittered in the filtered sunlight as he drained his glass of wine. Once more, Margaret wanted to look away and couldn't.

His voice was soft when he finally spoke. "Do you miss your husband?"

She sighed. "I did at first."

"And now?"

It was her turn to shrug. "I've adjusted. I've started a business and . . . a whole new life."

"Your business seems to be going well."

"Yes. It keeps me busy." She smiled. "And out of trouble."

He didn't return her smile. Instead he studied her gravely.

She shifted uncomfortably under his gaze. She searched her mind for something else to say. She felt relaxed when they were talking.

"Do you know what I'm thinking?" he said. There was a husky edge to his voice.

She shook her head slowly, once again mesmerized by his expression. She felt much the way she did when she stood on top of a ladder and looked down.

They stared at each other, and Margaret's heart began to beat in slow thuds.

The sensible part of Margaret, the part that had controlled her every action for the past twenty-seven years, screamed at her to get up and run. Run fast. And never look back.

"I'm thinking how very much I want to kiss you."

Margaret's voice sounded like someone else's when she finally answered him. "Then why don't you?"

Chapter Four

At first the kiss was the barest brushing of lips against lips, a gentle exploration, almost as if he were testing her to see if she'd really meant her invitation. Then Caleb placed his hands on her shoulders, pulled her closer and deepened the kiss.

Margaret's heart kicked into high gear, and the blood pounded in her veins as his tongue teased her mouth open and slipped inside.

If Margaret had felt as if she were drowning before, just by looking deep into Caleb's eyes, now she felt as if she'd been caught up in a whirlpool. Her head spun, and sensations assaulted her from all sides. She placed her hands on his chest, feeling his heat and strength under her palms.

Margaret stopped thinking. She simply absorbed. Her entire body felt as if it were slowly coming alive after a long, drugged sleep as Caleb's hands and mouth worked their magic. She wound her arms around his neck and gave herself up to the sensations rushing through her body.

Just as she had imagined when she'd thought about what it would be like to have him make love to her, his hands moved slowly. Their heat seared her as Caleb pulled her even closer, one hand slipping down until it caressed her bottom.

He wanted her. She could feel how much as he moved against her and his wet mouth dropped to her neck, nudging aside the collar of her blouse to burrow against her damp skin. His tongue flicked against her skin, trailing down into the swell of her bosom. Margaret trembled. The tremble gave way to a moan as his hands moved around to cup her breasts. She strained against him, wanting more. He gently ran his thumbs over the crests.

She whimpered as an exquisite pleasure rippled through her.

"Meggy," he said, his voice ragged. "Beautiful Meggy."

He made the name sound like an endearment. Margaret closed her eyes as he continued to stroke her. Finally he pulled her close and found her lips once more.

This kiss was greedy, demanding, insistent, and Margaret returned it with all the unspoken longings that had lain dormant for many years.

When they finally drew apart, he looked deep into her eyes, and she saw the blue fire of desire raging in their depths and knew her own eyes mirrored the same emotion.

He nuzzled her cheek and whispered, "I want to make love to you."

With those words, Margaret was catapulted back to reality. Panic careened through her. Her uncertainties and fears, momentarily forgotten by the strong physical attraction she felt for him, came rushing back in a torrent.

"Let's go to my place," he continued.

"No. No, I can't." She tried to pull away from him, but he held her fast.

"Why can't you?" He silenced her protest by kissing her hungrily. One hand held her head firmly, the other rotated in slow circles against her bottom, causing a sharp stab of desire to arc through her. "You want me," he muttered, his mouth moving to her ear. "I know you want me just as much as I want you." His tongue traced the curve of her ear, and Margaret shivered violently.

"See?" he said, holding her tightly against him.

Oh, yes, she wanted him. She wanted to say yes more than she'd wanted anything in a long time. She'd only had a taste of what it would be like to lie with Caleb, to have his slow hands move over her body, to feel the passion surge between them. And she wanted more than a taste. She wanted the entire meal. She wanted to gorge herself, to partake of every drop offered.

But she was scared. Scared of making a fool of herself. Scared she wouldn't measure up. She was also scared of being talked about. Laughed about. Oh, God. People were bound to find out, and then she'd be the town joke. She just couldn't. She couldn't. No matter how much she wanted to. There was too much at stake, too much to lose. Calling on the last of her willpower, she placed her hands on his chest and pushed him away. "I can't, Caleb. Please don't try to force me." She didn't even recognize her voice.

He dropped his hands as if she'd burned him. Regret and disappointment filled his eyes. "Lord, Margaret, I'd never force you. Is that what you think?"

"I'm sorry, I'm sorry. I don't know why I said that. Please don't be angry." Tears filled her eyes, and she blinked them back. Why had she said that? She was the one who'd invited his kiss. All she'd had to do was say no. She reached toward him, taking a deep breath to calm herself. "Please, Caleb. That was a rotten thing to say. I didn't mean it."

He sighed, then smiled crookedly, kissing the tip of her nose. "It's okay. I'm not angry. I *am* sorry, though. It would have been wonderful between us."

The tears Margaret had been fighting threatened to spill. She touched his cheek with trembling fingers. "I'm sorry, too," she whispered.

He clasped her hand against him, turning his face to kiss the open palm. Margaret closed her eyes. If only things were different. If only— She broke off the thought. Life was filled with "If onlys."

When she opened her eyes, he was looking at her, his face only inches away. She could see every small imperfection in his skin, the tiny bump in the bridge of his nose, his incredibly long eyelashes and his wonderful eyes. She wished she could stand here forever, just looking at him. Sadness for what could never be nearly overwhelmed her.

His eyes searched her face. "This isn't over between us, you know." His smile was tender. "No matter how you fight it, it's only beginning."

"Oh, Caleb, I don't think—"

"That's the trouble. You *are* thinking. You have to stop thinking. Learn to feel and follow those feelings."

His hand still clasped hers and he squeezed gently. "It's all right. I'll teach you."

"I—I'm not going to change my mind."

"Ah, Meggy, you'll change it. This thing between us is too strong to ignore. We both know that."

"No, Caleb—"

"You'll change it. Trust me. It might take awhile, but I'm a patient man. I can wait."

Oh, God. Her resistance was so low. If he continued to try to persuade her, she was afraid she'd give in. And then what? There'd be no way a liaison with Caleb could remain a secret in a small town like Riverview. How could she face her mother, her sister, her children, all the people she knew? She could just imagine what they'd all say, how they'd look, their knowing eyes. It would be unbearable.

At her expression, he chuckled. "Don't worry, sweet Meggy. I won't hound you." Then his smile faded and his voice gathered intensity. "Do you know why I won't hound you?"

Margaret shook her head slowly.

"Because when you finally come to me, I want you to come of your own free will. I want it to be a choice you make eagerly and happily. Without any reservations at all."

Caleb didn't arrive home until eight, because after he watched Margaret drive off, he climbed on his bike and headed for the countryside. He rode fast, letting the wind and speed of the bike cool his body as well as his desire.

As he rode, past rolling farmland and dense thickets of trees, around curves and up and down hills, he thought about Margaret. His reaction to her had stunned him. Caleb had had many women friends in the past. He'd had varying degrees of affection for each of them, varying degrees of passion toward them. None had ever affected him this way.

His feelings toward Margaret went beyond physical desire. Today, talking to her, listening to her, looking at her, he had felt an overwhelming urge to protect her. There was something so vulnerable and innocent about her, even though she was the most mature—and probably the most sensible—woman he'd ever dated.

Yet she had an almost childlike quality. Despite her marriage, despite her motherhood, Margaret seemed untouched.

Unawakened.

Yes, unawakened and uninitiated.

Just by the way she'd trembled in his arms, by the way she'd reacted to his kisses and his touch, Caleb knew Margaret was a woman who had never realized her full potential as a sexual being.

As the heat of the late summer day began to wane, and twilight purpled the sky, Caleb knew that just as Margaret had awakened protective urges in him—urges he'd never known he possessed—he wanted to awaken her.

By the time he reached the small brick carriage house he had called home the past seven years, he was determined to break down the barrier of Margaret's fears and doubts, no matter how long it took.

After showering off the dust from his bike ride, he put on his favorite faded cutoffs and an old sweatshirt with the sleeves torn out and fixed himself a fried bologna sandwich and a glass of milk. He carried his food into the living room and turned on the TV.

A cursory foray through the channels showed him there was nothing he wanted to watch. He thought about putting on some music—maybe Lyle Lovett—but didn't. He glanced at the newspaper while he ate his sandwich then, restless, got up and paced to the open windows.

He rarely turned on the air conditioning, even in midsummer. He hated being in a closed-up house, preferring to sweat a little and have the benefit of outside sounds and smells.

From his vantage point, he couldn't see much except the main house, which was dark. The owners, an elderly couple named Cornell and Hester Cameron, were on their yearly jaunt overseas—this time to Australia and New Zealand. Caleb idly wondered if they were having a good time. Then his thoughts segued to Margaret, and he wondered what it would be like to take a leisurely trip with her someplace where they didn't know anyone and no one knew them. He wondered if her fears would abate if she were away from inquisitive eyes. From there he wondered what she was doing right now, at this very moment. He glanced at the mantel clock. It was after nine.

He thought about calling her, then dismissed the urge. Too soon. He didn't want to crowd her or rush her. She would need tonight to think about what had happened between them, just as he was thinking about it. He'd call her tomorrow.

But the urge to talk to someone was strong. Someone he could tell about Margaret. He strode over to the phone and picked it up, pressing the familiar numbers of his favorite sister, Kathleen.

"Caleb! Hi! Haven't heard from you in a while. What's up?" Kathleen said upon hearing his voice. "Have you got a new girlfriend?"

"What do you mean?"

"Oh, come on, Caleb. You never call me unless you're in the first flush of a new love affair. So who is it this time?"

Caleb grimaced. "Promise not to lecture me."

"Oh, Caleb! You haven't gotten involved with a student! God, I've been afraid of this."

"Give me credit for some sense," he said, wounded by her inference. "I'd never get involved with a student."

"Well, thank God for that," Kathleen said. "So who is she then?"

"Would you believe a forty-five-year-old widow with three grown children and a grandchild on the way?"

There was silence for a long moment. Then she said, "You're serious."

"I'm very serious.

"Well, well, well, *this* is certainly different."

"I know."

"She must be something."

"She is. But probably not in the way you're thinking."

"Tell me about her."

So Caleb did. He started from the beginning, when he'd first seen Margaret, standing in the Richardson Center. "She looked so clean and attractive. She reminded me of that English actress, you know the one—from *Howard's End?*"

"Emma Thompson," Kathleen said.

"Yes, Emma Thompson. Margaret has that same quality about her. Classy, elegant, yet simple." He went on to describe the party and how he'd watched Margaret all night, how the more he'd watched her the more intrigued he became. He told Kathleen about his impulsive gesture in leaving the picnic basket on her doorstep, how he'd hoped Margaret would come. He told her about the picnic, although he left out the personal details.

Kathleen sighed when he was finished. "Hey, little brother, you sound smitten."

Caleb laughed self-consciously. "Do I?" Bewitched was a better word, he thought.

"So what're you going to do about her?"

"I don't know."

"Have you thought about the potential problems if you get involved with a woman like her? I mean, not only is she a recent widow, but she's got grown kids. I have a feeling her kids wouldn't look too kindly on their mother getting involved with someone like you."

He bristled. "What do you mean, *someone like me? What's wrong with me?*"

"Oh, Caleb, I'm sorry. I didn't mean it the way it sounded."

"Well, what did you mean?"

"I just meant, you know. You're younger than she is, and you've, well, you've got to admit your track record isn't all that great."

"Now, wait a minute, Kath. What the hell's gotten into you? You're making me sound like—"

"Like a guy who takes his pleasure and walks away without a backward glance?"

Her insinuation hung in the air for a long moment. Caleb wanted to say she was being unfair, yet deep in his heart he knew Kathleen was only stating the truth. Loving them and leaving them had been his past history. "Look," he finally said, "maybe I have, but I've never lied to anyone. They always knew exactly how I felt. The choices were always theirs to make."

"Yes, I know. I also know you've prided yourself on your honesty and frankness with every woman you've ever been involved with." Her voice grew softer. "But, Caleb, you know you've left a string of broken hearts."

He opened his mouth to refute her accusation. The charge stung, yet even as he started to counter, he knew she had again spoken the truth. He'd never wanted to hurt anyone, yet he had. He'd justified his actions by telling himself that each time he had been upfront about his feelings. He had told each woman that he wasn't interested in long-term commitment, and they had gladly gone along with his terms. A couple had even echoed his terms, saying this is what they wanted, too. Yet in the end, there had rarely been a casual parting.

Kathleen's voice remained soft as she spoke again. "This Margaret, she's probably very vulnerable, Caleb."

"Yes."

"She could get hurt. Is that what you want?"

"No. No, I don't want that at all."

"Then be careful," his sister said. "Think a long time before you go any further with this involvement. Be sure you can handle the consequences."

Margaret didn't sleep well. She dreamed, fitful dreams filled with images of Anthony and the children and then, toward morning, of Caleb and their picnic. The dream made no sense, and when her alarm went off at nine o'clock, she didn't feel rested.

An hour later, after a couple of cups of coffee and a long shower, she felt much better. She dressed carefully for church. She sang in the choir and would don a choir robe, but she usually went out for lunch with Rosemary after the service and liked to look her best. The two women had fallen into the habit of lunching together after Anthony died, and both looked forward to it.

As Margaret drove toward the church, she wondered if anyone would mention her date with Caleb yesterday. If she were lucky, no one would have heard about it yet. She wasn't sure she was up to defending herself with her mother.

Throughout the service, Margaret imagined that people were looking at her speculatively. When the service was over and the last hymn sung, she walked back to the dressing room and dawdled over removing her robe. Finally she knew she'd have to go outside. Her mother would not leave the grounds without at least saying hello.

She made her way through the congregation, some of whom still lingered inside the vestibule.

"Good morning, Margaret."

"Hello, Margaret."

"Nice hymns today, Margaret."

She nodded and smiled and murmured greetings back to each person who spoke.

Reverend Donnelly smiled at her as she walked past on her way out the door. She spied Rosemary off to the right, talking to a young couple who had just moved to Riverview. Rosemary waved, and Margaret waved back. As Margaret descended the steps, she saw her mother break away from a cluster of people off to the left of the broad sidewalk.

Joyce Guthrie looked immaculate, as always, in a violet linen dress, ivory-colored hose and matching pumps. Her gray hair, which still carried a strong hint of blond, was perfectly coiffed, not a strand out of place. As tall as Margaret, who stood five-five in her stocking feet, Joyce carried herself proudly. Her green eyes hadn't dimmed over the years. They could still strike terror in the heart of her oldest daughter.

"Good morning, Margaret," her mother said as they drew abreast.

"Good morning, Mother."

Joyce's clear eyes narrowed a bit as she studied Margaret. "You look tired. Aren't you sleeping well?"

"I'm sleeping just fine."

"Are you drinking your warm milk? And watching your sugar intake? Eating sugar before bedtime isn't conducive to a good night's rest."

Margaret sighed. "Honestly, Mother, I'm a grown woman. I know what I should and shouldn't eat."

"Perhaps you should let Madelyn take a look at you."

The last thing Margaret wanted to do was be scrutinized by her sister. "I've told you before. I don't feel comfortable going to Madelyn."

Joyce shook her head. "Why you'd prefer going to a stranger, and an *outsider,* at that, I'll never know."

"Dr. Trucksis is a wonderful doctor," Margaret said automatically, as she had dozens of times before. "He can also be objective."

"But Madelyn is *family.*"

"Mother, can we please not argue?" Margaret said. Her head was beginning to ache, something that happened almost every time she talked to her mother. "Besides, I think Rosemary is ready to go."

Unperturbed, Joyce said, "Come along and say hello to your aunt Louise before you take off with Rosemary."

Margaret started to say she had intended to do so, then stopped. What was the use? Her mother was her mother, and she'd never treat Margaret any differently, no matter what Margaret said.

"Hello, Margaret," her aunt said, walking toward her. She kissed Margaret's cheek.

"Hi, Aunt Louise." Margaret returned the affectionate caress fondly. Louise Jannett, Joyce's sister, was as unlike Joyce as two women could be. Warm and loving, Louise had always made Margaret wish she could have been her daughter instead.

"That's a beautiful outfit," Louise said, looking with approval at Margaret's tailored beige silk suit. "It looks great on you."

"Thanks," Margaret said, smiling with pleasure. "It's new."

"You've been buying a lot of clothes lately, haven't you?" her mother said.

Margaret gritted her teeth. Why was it that no matter what her mother said to her it sounded like a criticism? "I've bought a few," she replied mildly.

"You should be careful of your money, Margaret," Joyce said. "It's got to last you a long time. Isn't that right, Louise?" She looked to her sister for support.

"Oh, Joyce, Margaret's not a spendthrift," Louise said, giving Margaret another smile.

"She never *used* to be," Joyce said.

A dozen retorts to her mother's implied criticism sprang to Margaret's mind, and she forced them all back. All she said was, "You don't have to worry about me." She looked around for Rosemary, wishing her friend would rescue her.

"What did you do yesterday afternoon?" her mother said. "I tried to call you several times, and there was never any answer."

"I...uh...had some errands to run." Margaret could feel herself flushing. Why had she lied? Her mother was bound to find out about the picnic with Caleb, and Margaret's lie would only make things worse. "Did you want me for something special?"

Her mother's eyes seemed to narrow. "No. Do I have to have a reason to call my daughter?"

"No, of course not, Mother. I just thought..." Margaret let her voice trail off and looked in Rosemary's direction once again. As she did, Rosemary looked her way, and Margaret sent her a frantic signal with her eyes. Rosemary grinned, said something to the young couple, then walked purposefully toward Margaret.

"Hello, Mrs. Guthrie, Mrs. Jannett," she said as she drew near.

"Good morning, Rosemary," said Joyce, eyeing Rosemary's teal dress and matching picture hat. Margaret knew her mother was adding up the cost of each item Rosemary wore.

"Hello, Rosemary," said Louise. "Are you and Margaret going to The Inn for lunch today?"

"Uh-huh, and if we don't get going, we'll be late." Rosemary glanced at her watch, then met Margaret's gaze. Her dark eyes twinkled knowingly. "I made our reservations for twelve forty-five."

Margaret gratefully began saying her goodbyes, and just as she and Rosemary had almost made good their escape, Phyllis Dixon, a bridge partner of Margaret's mother and the town's worst gossip, came rushing over.

"Well, *hello,* everyone. Louise. Joyce. Rosemary. And *Margaret,*" she gushed. "What's this I hear about *you?*" Her bright eyes fastened on Margaret, and her round face, which had always reminded Margaret of a kewpie doll, slid into a sly smile.

"Hello, Phyllis," Margaret said, resigned to the worst.

"Hi, Phyllis," Rosemary said. "Sorry we can't talk. Margaret and I have reservations for lunch, and we've really got to be going."

But Phyllis, hot on the heels of her prey, wasn't to be deterred so easily. She gripped Margaret's forearm, and short of making a scene, Margaret was forced to stand still.

Self-satisfaction oozing from each word, Phyllis cocked one eyebrow and said, "I hear you were having a *very* cozy picnic in the park yesterday afternoon." She paused dramatically. "With a *very* handsome young man." She shot a smug look at Joyce.

Margaret avoided her mother's eyes and wished fervently that she could strangle Phyllis. She searched frantically for a reply and came up with nothing.

"Well, come on, Margaret," Phyllis said happily, "don't keep us in suspense! Just who was he?"

Chapter Five

"You wouldn't know him," Margaret said as off-handedly as she could manage.

"Try me," Phyllis retorted.

On second thought, maybe strangling was too good for Phyllis. "He's just a friend," Margaret said firmly, then because she couldn't avoid it any longer, she finally met her mother's gaze.

Joyce's expression revealed nothing, yet Margaret knew her mother was as avidly curious as Phyllis. But Joyce Guthrie didn't believe in showing emotion of any kind, especially not to outsiders. Family unity was all important, she believed.

"You're being evasive, Margaret," Phyllis said, wagging her index finger in Margaret's face and letting loose with one of her giggles, which had always reminded Margaret of a hen's cackle. "Isn't she, Joyce?"

If Phyllis Dixon had thought Joyce would support her in her quest for information, Margaret knew the woman was going to be disappointed. No matter what Margaret's mother thought, she would close ranks when it came to the privacy of her family.

"Really, Phyllis, your nosiness knows no bounds," Joyce said, raising her chin and looking down her nose in her haughtiest manner.

Margaret smothered a smile, even though she knew she wasn't off the hook. She'd have to face her mother's questions later.

"Nosy! I'm not nosy! Why, I'm just *interested* in Margaret, that's all." Phyllis gave Joyce a mock wounded look, but her eyes betrayed her with their hungry glitter.

"Sorry to break up this fascinating conversation," Rosemary interjected smoothly, "but Margaret and I really have to go."

"Yes, we do," Margaret said. She smiled at her mother. "Goodbye, Aunt Louise...nice seeing you, Phyllis."

Phyllis opened her mouth to say something else, but Joyce interrupted. "You two have fun," she said. Her gaze met Margaret's levelly. "Margaret, call me when you get home."

Five minutes later, safely on their way to brunch in Rosemary's sporty little almond-colored car, Rosemary said, "I thought you weren't going to go on that picnic with Caleb Mahoney."

Margaret made a face. "So did I."

Rosemary started to laugh. "Gawd, did you *see* Phyllis Dixon's face when she collared you? She practically wet her pants she was so excited to find out who you were with."

Margaret laughed, too. "I know. It gave me great pleasure to thwart her." Her laughter subsided, and she sighed. "Unfortunately there'll be no thwarting my mother."

"Yeah, I heard her ordering you to call her. But you didn't really expect to keep the picnic a secret, did you?"

"No. Not in this town."

"Well, come on, tell me about it. I want to know every last juicy detail."

"Okay, *Phyllis.*"

Rosemary grimaced. "Damn. I *did* sound like her, didn't I?"

"No, you didn't. I was just teasing you, that's all."

They fell silent for a long moment, then Rosemary said, "Well? Are you going to tell me or not?"

When Margaret had related everything she remembered about the picnic, she said softly, "I let him kiss me, Ro. I know I shouldn't have."

"Why not?" Rosemary grinned. "If it'd been me, I'd have probably let him kiss me, too."

"Yes, but you're not in mourning, and you don't have anyone to answer to. I worried all night that maybe someone saw us and the whole town would know."

Rosemary reached over and squeezed Margaret's knee. "Quit worrying, Magpie. You're a grown woman. If you wanted him to kiss you, you had a perfect right to let him."

"I just . . . I don't know . . . I can't help but feel as if I did something wrong."

"You did nothing wrong."

"Then why do I feel guilty?"

"That's easy. It's your nature to feel guilty when you do anything you think anyone might disapprove of.

That's been your biggest problem your whole life. You try to make everybody happy, and believe me, that's not possible." Rosemary slanted her a sideways look. "How many times have I told you that the only person you can make happy is yourself?"

Margaret sighed. "I know, I know." She bit her bottom lip and wondered if she should confide everything to Rosemary. She sorely needed someone's advice, and Rosemary was the most sensible person she knew.

"So are you planning to see him again?" Rosemary asked. She braked for a red light and turned to Margaret, her dark eyes sympathetic and understanding.

Margaret shook her head, and a feeling of sadness gripped her. "No."

"Why not?" Rosemary grinned, her eyes twinkling. "Didn't you like the way he kissed?"

Even Rosemary's teasing didn't make Margaret feel better. "I liked it too much."

"Ahh."

"I'm afraid to see him again," Margaret added softly. "I don't trust myself."

"I see."

"Do you?"

"I think so. If I'm reading you correctly, you want to see him again, but you're afraid you might succumb to the sexy professor's not-inconsiderable charms, which would be disastrous because you're not the type to settle for a love affair, and he's not the type to want anything permanent, plus he's younger than you are, which wouldn't bother him, but probably bothers you—" She broke off to take a breath, then added, "And you're afraid of what everyone will say about you—the perfectly proper Mrs. Desmond. Does that about sum it up?"

Margaret nodded glumly. "In a nutshell."

By now they'd reached the Riverview Inn, which was the oldest, as well as the nicest, restaurant in Riverview, and Rosemary pulled in under the porte cochere. A valet parking attendant opened the passenger door, and Margaret allowed him to help her out. She waited while Rosemary gave her keys to the other attendant, then the two women walked up the three broad stone steps leading into the interior of the vintage 1914 inn.

A pretty, redheaded hostess led them to their window table overlooking a small private lake stocked with swans. The water looked cool and green and peaceful. The inn was set in a wooded park filled with flowers and trails and was a popular setting for outdoor weddings. Colorful peacocks roamed the grounds, and squirrels scampered everywhere. At night, thousands of tiny white lights twinkled from the branches of the trees, lending a fairy-tale quality to the setting and reminding Margaret of Tavern on the Green in Central Park, which she was sure the owners had emulated.

After their water glasses were filled and they'd placed their orders, Rosemary said, "What're you going to tell your mother when you talk to her?"

Margaret shrugged. "The truth, I guess. What choice do I have? She'll find out, anyway."

Rosemary nodded. "Don't let her put you on the defensive about it. You did nothing wrong."

Margaret sighed. "The trouble is, right before Phyllis zoomed down on her broomstick this morning, Mother asked me where I was yesterday afternoon. She said she'd tried to call me several times. And I . . . uh, I lied to her. I told her I was out running errands. The minute the words were out of my mouth, I could have kicked myself." She met Rosemary's gaze. "I don't know why I lied. It was stupid."

Rosemary grimaced. "Lying might have been ill-advised, but it's certainly understandable. Your mother's a formidable woman."

"I can't imagine you dodging the truth, no matter who was doing the asking." Margaret ran her index finger across the condensation on her water glass. "I'm a coward."

"You're *not* a coward, Magpie. You just don't like confrontations. It's like I said before. You think it's your mission in life to make everyone happy. It's a quality I really admire, even though sometimes I wish you'd just tell everyone to go to hell."

Margaret smiled, Rosemary's loyalty warming her heart. "Even you?" she teased.

"With the exception of your dearest friend, of course," Rosemary added, laughing, "who never, *ever*, oversteps the bounds of friendship."

Suddenly serious, Margaret said, "You know you can ask me anything."

Rosemary took a sip of her water, studying Margaret over the rim of the glass. After a moment, she said softly, "Do you *want* to see Caleb again, Margaret?"

"I thought you'd already decided I do."

"I have been known to be wrong on occasion."

"You're not wrong this time."

"But you're not going to."

"No."

"Good."

"So you think I've made the right decision."

Just then their waiter approached, and Rosemary waited for him to serve them before answering. "Yes, I do think you've made the right decision, but not because of what anyone might think about you going out with him. I told you yesterday, I don't want to see you get hurt.''

Margaret picked up her fork and took a bite of her peppered shrimp and eggs, a specialty of the house. ''I don't want to get hurt, either.'' She looked up.

Rosemary's dark eyes were solemn as they met hers. ''Then don't change your mind, Magpie. Stay as far away from Caleb Mahoney as you can get.''

Margaret put off calling her mother for a good hour after she arrived home. Finally, though, she knew she could delay no longer. She steeled herself and picked up the phone.

Her mother answered on the second ring.

''Hello, Mother,'' Margaret said.

''Hello, Margaret. Did you have a nice lunch?''

''Yes, very nice.''

There was a moment of silence, then Joyce said, ''Why did you lie to me when I asked you where you were yesterday afternoon?''

Margaret sighed wearily. ''The truth, Mother?''

''Certainly the truth,'' Joyce said indignantly.

''I knew you wouldn't approve, and I wanted to avoid this very discussion. I know that was cowardly of me, and I'm sorry.''

''If you knew I wouldn't approve, you must have been doing something you shouldn't have been doing.''

Why did her mother always have to sound so certain about everything? So coldly superior? ''It was just a picnic with a friend. There's nothing wrong with that.'' But even as she said the words, Margaret thought about Caleb's kisses, his touches and the way she'd acted, and she knew her face was blazing. Thank God, this discussion was taking place over the phone instead of in person. If her mother could see her face, she'd immediately know Margaret had done many things yesterday she shouldn't have.

"Who is this friend?" Joyce demanded.

Margaret gritted her teeth. She wished she had nerve enough to say it wasn't any of her mother's business, just as her mother had rebuked Phyllis earlier in the day. "He's an English professor at the university."

"An English professor at the university," Joyce repeated. "What's his name?"

"You wouldn't know him, Mother."

"You act as if you don't want me to know his name. Is there something wrong with him?"

Margaret knew her mother's tenacity when she wanted something. She might as well tell her what she wanted to know, take her lumps, then try to forget about yesterday and Caleb. "There's nothing wrong with him. His name is Caleb Mahoney."

"And how did you meet him?"

"I met him at Dean Anderson's house Friday night."

"I thought you were working at that party."

Margaret sighed again. "I *was* working at the party. But I also met some of the guests. Catherine Higgins was there."

If Margaret had hoped to sidetrack her mother, her hope was shortlived.

"Did Catherine introduce you to this Professor Mahoney?"

Deciding she'd been a spineless wimp long enough, Margaret squared her shoulders and said firmly, "No. He introduced himself. Now you know everything. So can we please drop this discussion?"

"I still have some things I want to say."

Margaret closed her eyes and counted to ten.

"It is unseemly and entirely inappropriate for you to be dating anyone so soon after your husband's death. You do realize that, don't you, Margaret?"

"Anthony's been dead eight months, Mother. And it wasn't a *date,* it was a picnic."

"To show proper respect, a widow should wait at least a year before going out with a male friend, whether it's a date or a picnic or whatever you choose to call it."

"All right! You've made your point."

"It isn't necessary to shout at me, Margaret," her mother said icily.

Margaret forced herself to lower her voice and speak calmly. "I'm sorry. I didn't mean to shout. It's just that—"

"I'm only thinking of your welfare, you know." Joyce's stiff tone communicated her wounded feelings, and Margaret felt a familiar guilt consume her.

"I know that, Mother. But you don't have to worry. I'm not going anywhere with Professor Mahoney again."

"That's good." Joyce's tone softened. "Because really, dear, you're in a vulnerable state right now. Still mourning dear Anthony. And you're a prime target for some man to take advantage of. You have to be careful, you know. Anthony left you very nicely situated, and there are all sorts of unscrupulous—"

"Caleb isn't like that!"

There was a long silence, during which Margaret wished she could bite off her tongue. Why hadn't she just kept quiet, let her mother say whatever she wanted to say? What harm would it have done? After all, it wasn't as if Caleb would ever know that Joyce had insulted him.

"Just how old is this Caleb?" her mother finally said, all the softness gone.

"Mother, I don't want to offend you or make you mad, but I don't wish to discuss this any longer. How old he is doesn't matter, because I told you, I'm not going to see him again. Now, if you don't mind, I've got to go. I'm going over to Lisa's, and I don't want to be late."

Margaret had lied to her mother again. She wasn't going over to Lisa's house until five, and it was only three-thirty when she hung up the phone. She didn't care, though. She was tired of trying to explain her actions to her mother. Tired of being treated like a child and being subjected to criticism at every turn.

Tears stung her eyes as she walked into her sunny living room. She fought the feelings her mother had generated and stood there for a moment, trying to decide what she wanted to do with the rest of the afternoon. Just as she had decided she would change into old clothes and spend the next hour working in the yard, the phone rang.

She sighed wearily. What now? Had her mother thought of some other shortcoming to lecture her about?

She reluctantly picked up the extension in the hall. "Hello?"

"Hello, Meggy."

Margaret's mouth went dry at the sound of Caleb's husky voice. "Hello, Caleb." She fought to keep her own voice from betraying her emotions.

"I've been thinking about you ever since you left the park yesterday." His voice was like an intimate caress as it slid over her body.

Knees suddenly gone weak, Margaret sat down. Not trusting herself to speak, she tried to calm her erratic heartbeat by taking a deep, shaky breath.

"I wanted to call you last night," he continued, his voice filled with intimacy and reminders of yesterday. "But I thought it might be best to give you some time."

Margaret swallowed. For a long moment, silence vibrated between them. Then, the timbre of his voice deepening even further, he said, "Do you believe in destiny, Meggy?"

Margaret closed her eyes. "I don't know," she whispered.

"I do," he said. "I believe some things are preordained, that no matter what we do, or how we struggle against them, they're meant to happen."

"Caleb—"

"That's what I think happened with us," he continued determinedly, just as if she hadn't spoken. "I think we were destined to meet." Then he laughed softly. "I also think we're destined to have dinner together tonight."

Margaret wished she could think of something clever and lighthearted to say. But right now she didn't feel clever or lighthearted. All she felt was infinitely sad and achingly empty. Pushing away the impossible yearning that filled her, she said, "I'm sorry, Caleb. I can't have dinner with you tonight."

"Ah, sweet Meggy, of course you can. It's easy. All you have to do is say yes."

Margaret could hear the smile in his voice, the tenderness, and she wished with all her heart she could throw caution to the wind, say to hell with everything and everyone, follow her impulses and let them take her where they would.

But visions of her mother's coldly implacable eyes, her children and her coming grandchild, Phyllis Dixon and others of her breed, all stopped her.

No one would understand. They would all censure her. She would be a pariah. A joke. People would laugh at her. Say she had lost her mind. Say she was trying to recapture her youth. No! She couldn't bear it, couldn't bear the whispers and sly innuendo.

"Come on, Meggy, say yes."

"I already have plans for this evening," she said.

"Oh."

He sounded so disappointed, she couldn't help the feeling of gratification that washed over her. Nor could she help explaining. "I'm going over to my daughter's house for dinner."

"Oh! Well, then, how about tomorrow night?" he said enthusiastically, all traces of disappointment gone.

"No, really, Caleb, I can't." Margaret ignored the regret for what couldn't be and took a deep breath. "I've been thinking about you a lot since yesterday, too."

"Well, that's a step in the right direction," he said with amusement.

"And I've decided that I'm not going to see you again."

He was silent for so long, Margaret wasn't sure he'd heard her. "Caleb?" she said softly. "Are you still there?"

"Yes, I'm still here."

"Then why don't you say something?"

"What do you want me to say?"

Margaret sighed in frustration. He wasn't going to make this easy. "I want you to say you respect my decision and that it's okay, there are no hard feelings. Then I want you to say goodbye and not call me again."

"Well, Meggy, I'm sorry to disappoint you, but that's not going to happen, because I can't accept your decision. I can't believe that this is what you really want."

Please, please... "I have to go now, Caleb," Margaret said, desperation fueling her resolve.

"All right, Margaret," he said with quiet gravity. "I'll let you go, but only if you'll promise me something."

"What?" she said suspiciously.

"Promise me you'll have dinner with me tomorrow night."

"Caleb, I told you—"

"I know what you told me, and if, after spending the evening with me tomorrow, you still feel the same way, I won't pressure you anymore. I'll accept your decision, and you won't hear from me again."

Margaret knew she shouldn't. But the temptation to see him again, just one more time, was too great. She told herself that one time couldn't hurt anything. Besides, she could make him understand she'd meant what she'd said if she told him in person. "You're sure you'll accept my decision?"

"Absolutely sure."

"I'm not going to change my mind," she warned.

"Fine. Whatever you say."

Margaret sighed. "All right. Tomorrow night."

"Good," he said matter-of-factly. "I'll come by for you at seven. That's not too early, is it?"

"No, that's not too early. You don't expect me to ride on your motorcycle, do you?"

"No, Mrs. Desmond, I do not expect you to ride on my motorcycle. I also own a car."

"That's good," she said with relief. She could just imagine what her neighbors would think if she climbed onto the back of a motorcycle. Why, if her mother heard about it, she'd try to have Margaret committed!

"Oh, and wear something casual," he said offhandedly, just as if he wasn't throwing a bomb at her, "because we'll be having dinner here, at my place."

"Th-there?" Her heart gave a treacherous leap.

He chuckled. "You sound frightened, Meggy."

"I'm not frightened." Of course she wasn't frightened. She didn't intend to do anything other than have dinner and talk. Why should she be frightened?

And actually, she guessed having dinner at his house would be better than going out. There would be less chance of anyone seeing them together.

Yes, dinner at his house was a good plan. "I'm not frightened at all," she said again, more firmly this time.

"I'm certainly glad of that. And I'll tell you what," he added. "To put your mind completely at ease, I'll make you a promise, too. I promise not to do anything tomorrow night that you don't want me to do. Now, see? If you *had* happened to be frightened, there wouldn't have been any reason to be."

Chapter Six

Caleb stared thoughtfully at the phone after he hung up from talking to Margaret. He wondered if she had any idea of the feelings she aroused in him. Even now, just hearing her voice had filled him with an aching tenderness.

He knew he had frightened her. Yesterday, when they'd kissed and she hadn't been able to disguise her own rising passion. And again today, when he'd talked about destiny.

He still couldn't quite believe he'd said all those things to her. He'd sounded like some kind of sappy, lovesick fool spouting off like that. Destiny! Damn, what had gotten into him?

But how else to explain this feeling of *inevitability* that struck him every time he was around Margaret? He knew his feelings defied logic, but he also knew that something had caused Margaret to cross his path, something more than pure chance. Caleb wasn't particularly religious and usually scoffed at things like astrology and palm reading, but at that moment he knew, as surely as he knew his own name, that what he'd told Margaret was the absolute truth.

They were meant to be together.

To be lovers.

And she knew it, too.

That's why Caleb had felt no qualms over making his promise to her. His promise to do nothing she didn't want him to do would not stop their relationship from progressing to its foregone conclusion. No, from the moment they'd met, from the moment he'd gazed into her beautiful amber eyes, with their beguiling look of innocence, the two of them had been like two trains hurtling toward each other on the same track, powerless to stop the inevitable collision.

Caleb sucked in his breath as he imagined the explosive meeting. He actually had to shake himself to get rid of the mental picture but it didn't stop the uncontrolled physical response of his body, and he gave a rueful laugh. "I think you're sorely in need of a cold shower!"

Margaret took a cold shower after grubbing away in the hot sun for more than an hour. The coolness felt wonderful on her heated skin. When she was finished she felt refreshed and as ready as she'd ever be to face several hours in the company of Lisa's in-laws.

Lisa and Keith lived in a new subdivision on the other side of Riverview from Margaret, but it took Margaret less than fifteen minutes to get there. In a town of twenty-one thousand people, the distances weren't great no matter what your destination.

"Hi, Mom," Lisa said, opening the front door to Margaret's knock.

Margaret smiled at her oldest daughter. "Hi, honey." The two hugged.

As the two drew apart, Lisa grinned and patted her rounded belly. "Boy, Krista has really been active today," she said happily.

Margaret thought her daughter looked even more beautiful pregnant than she'd looked before. Lisa was one of those fortunate women who never felt sick, whose skin bloomed and whose eyes glowed. Although she was finally beginning to show now, in her fifth month, she wasn't at all ungainly or awkward yet.

Lisa inclined her head toward the back of the new split-level home that had been custom-built by her father-in-law's construction company. "Everyone's in the sun room. C'mon back," she said, leading the way.

Margaret followed behind, admiring, as she always did, Lisa's crisp good looks. She was lucky, Margaret thought, having inherited the best of both Anthony's and her own genes. Lisa's hair was as golden blond as Anthony's had been, and her eyes were the same clear green as her grandmother Guthrie's. Tall and slender, she had a creamy complexion dusted with freckles.

Her only flaw—which Margaret didn't consider a flaw at all—was nearsightedness. But Lisa constantly bemoaned the fact that, for some reason, she couldn't wear contact lenses, and had to wear glasses. To compensate for this imagined defect, she owned at least a dozen pairs of glasses in different colors.

Today she wore huge round ones with candy-apple red frames, a perfect accessory for her peppermint striped maternity top and matching shorts. On her slender feet were red sandals.

They entered the sun room and Margaret smiled her greetings, turning first to Lisa's mother-in-law. Dolly Hubbard was always exquisitely turned out, and today was no exception, Margaret saw, taking in Dolly's expensive-looking royal blue slacks and matching silk shirt.

"It's nice to see you, Margaret," Dolly said. "We don't see each other nearly often enough."

"Yes, I know," Margaret said, thinking it was often enough to suit her.

"Margaret!" Floyd Hubbard boomed, standing to envelop her in a bear hug, which Margaret stoically endured. "You sure look pretty today," he said as he released her. "I *sure* do like a woman in a dress." His eyes raked her admiringly, lingering on the neckline of her yellow cotton sundress just a moment too long for Margaret's comfort. She had worn a dress because when she wore shorts he always stared at her legs, and when she wore slacks he kept eyeing her rump. She wondered how Dolly could stand him. Then, cynically, she thought that for some women, money compensated for a multitude of sins.

Keith, Lisa's tall, rather shy, husband—who hadn't seemed to inherit any of his parents' less than admirable traits—kissed her cheek in greeting and gave her a warm smile.

Margaret sat in a wicker chair a few feet from Dolly and as far from Floyd as she could manage. She resisted the impulse to pull the front of her sundress up, even though it was cut modestly high, and the straps over the shoulders were at least three inches wide.

"What would you like to drink, Mom?" Lisa asked. "Dolly and Floyd are having margaritas, and—" She grimaced. "I'm having lemonade."

"I'm having lemonade, too, honey," Keith said. From the onset of Lisa's pregnancy, he'd given up alcohol along with her.

Margaret thought again how sweet he was. Maybe he was adopted. "I'll have a margarita, too." She thought she'd probably need one to cope with the Hubbards. Turning to Dolly, she said, "How have you been, Dolly?"

The woman sighed. "Extremely busy, as usual. You know how involved I am with my club. Somedays I just don't know if I'm coming or going." She raised her right hand and patted her sleek brown hair. Margaret saw the enormous sapphire rimmed with diamonds on her ring finger and knew the older woman had intended for her to see it.

"That's a lovely ring," Margaret commented dutifully. "Is it new?"

Dolly beamed. "Yes, Floyd gave it to me last week. For no reason at all. Isn't that just like him?"

Margaret decided Dolly was either the best actress in the world or incredibly stupid, because if Margaret, who was usually the last to know anything, knew that Floyd always gifted his wife with an expensive jewel when he was feeling guilty about a new affair, everyone else in Riverview knew it, too. At least Anthony hadn't done anything so obvious.

As soon as the thought slid through her mind, Margaret banished it. She had promised herself years ago, when she'd decided she didn't intend to break up their home over Anthony's unfaithfulness, that she would never think of it. And now, after he was dead, there was no point in reminding herself that she had no room to criticize anyone, even the hapless Dolly.

We all cope in the best way we know how, she thought sadly. She shook off her dismal thoughts as she realized Floyd was talking to her.

"I was disappointed you didn't come to the hearing Wednesday night, Margaret," he said.

Margaret belatedly remembered that a representative from the State Zoning Commission had been scheduled to listen to both sides of the issue concerning the building of the proposed airport. "I forgot all about it," she admitted, then asked politely, "how did it go?"

Anthony, along with Floyd and a couple of other cohorts, had been a driving force behind the committee, and Margaret knew she was expected to continue to support their fight to get the commission to rezone the lands just west of the city so the proposed airport could be built.

The thing was, Margaret secretly agreed with the environmentalists who wanted to keep the bird refuge intact. She couldn't understand why Floyd and his committee couldn't find another site—one that wouldn't disturb the delicate balance of nature. She also knew she'd never hear the end of it if she said so.

"Damned bureaucrats!" Floyd said, his broad face flushing. "The guy the commission sent seemed to sympathize with that bunch of bleeding hearts, most of 'em those damned university people. Thing that burns me up is most of those eggheads aren't even from around here, anyway! They shouldn't have a say in what we do." Floyd drained his margarita and held the empty glass out to Keith. "Son, I'll have another one."

Keith took the glass.

"Damned idiots," Floyd muttered. "They're all sitting in their safe, tenured jobs, so what do they care about progress? That airport would create jobs for people, bring a lot of money into our town, but do they care? Hell, no, they don't care about *people!* They care about goddamned *birds!* Too many goddamned birds around now, anyway.''

Dolly rolled her eyes. ''Floyd, can't you talk about anything *else?*'' she complained. ''And do you have to *swear* so much?''

Floyd ignored his wife and reached for his new drink as Keith approached. Margaret hoped he'd forget about the airport controversy. She'd heard it all before.

''We're going to Germany next month,'' Dolly chirped, sounding for all the world like one of those birds Floyd was so adamant about.

''How nice,'' Margaret said, turning to Dolly and trying not to smile at her wicked thought.

''I'll bet if we were planning to put some kind of bleeding heart, low-income housing project out there, those damned university people wouldn't be complaining! It's just because they think we're going to make *money* off this project that they've gotten in an uproar. They act like a little good, honest capitalism is a dirty word. Damned communists!'' Floyd said, hitting the arm of his chair for emphasis.

''Floyd!'' said Dolly, obviously exasperated. ''I'm sick of hearing about this, and I'm sure Margaret and the kids are, too.''

Floyd glared at his wife. ''You're sick of it because you don't care about anything except spending money and gossiping.''

Dolly's face hardened, and she seemed about to retort, then subsided into icy silence.

Margaret decided the next time Lisa invited her over when the Hubbards were going to be there, she would make up some excuse. Then, with a sinking feeling, she realized that once the baby was born, she would not be able to avoid them. The baby would be their grandchild, too, and she was sure they'd be doting grandparents. Oh, yes, the three of them were bound to be thrown together at every opportunity. Margaret glumly pictured a long succession of holidays and birthdays for years to come.

For the rest of the evening, the thought niggled at Margaret. She hadn't quite realized, when Lisa married, that her children's in-laws would of necessity be cast into her sphere, like it or not.

Thank goodness Tony's in-laws didn't live in Riverview, she thought, feeling absurdly grateful to her son for his completely unintentional thoughtfulness and consideration in marrying a girl from Connecticut.

By the time the Hubbards said their goodbyes, Margaret felt exhausted with the effort of smiling and talking to people she didn't much like. She couldn't wait to get home.

"'Night, Mom," Lisa said as she walked her to the front door. "See you tomorrow night."

"Oh," Margaret said. "I'm afraid I won't be able to make bible class this week, honey."

"Oh, well." Lisa smiled. "Your business comes first, I know."

Margaret decided it wasn't really lying not to correct Lisa's mistaken assumption that she had a job the following evening.

But as she drove slowly home, she knew it was a darned good thing tomorrow night would be the last time she saw Caleb, because if nothing else, the fact that seeing him had caused her, in the space of less than twelve hours, to lie twice to her mother and once to her daughter, would have been proof enough she'd made the right decision.

"Hey, Caleb, wait up!"

Caleb turned and saw Jake Byo, his best friend, loping toward him. At six feet seven, Jake looked as if he should be a basketball player. No one, seeing him in his jeans, high tops and striped rugby shirt would peg him for a teacher of Elizabethan drama.

"Why're you in such a hurry?" Jake said as he drew abreast and fell into step with Caleb.

"I've got a date tonight." Caleb had had a hard time concentrating on his classes today. He kept eyeing his watch and thinking about Margaret, and by the end of the afternoon, he was itching to get home and start his dinner preparations.

Jake grinned. "Who is it this time? That new waitress at The Elmton? Or are you still seeing Alice Ann?"

"Neither," Caleb said. Although he usually told Jake all about his women friends, he felt curiously reluctant to talk to him about Margaret.

By now the two men had reached the faculty parking lot, and Caleb stopped by his bike. Jake stopped, too. "Caleb," he said slowly, "do you ever think about... getting married?"

"Who, me?" Caleb said, grinning. "I'm not the marrying kind, you know that. Why?" Then his eyes widened in amazement. "Are *you* thinking about getting married?"

Jake gave him a sheepish look. "Yeah, well..."

"I don't believe it! Marilyn finally talked you into it, huh?" Marilyn Kenny, a local realtor, had been Jake's girlfriend for almost two years, and Caleb knew she'd been putting some pressure on Jake the past few months.

Jake shrugged. "It was a mutual decision."

"Are you sure? You don't look very happy about it."

"It's not that." He gave Caleb a shy smile. "I know it took me awhile to realize what I wanted, but I know now. I really want to marry Marilyn. It's just that...well, she wants a church wedding...you know, the works, and I just wish we could take off for Vegas or something."

Caleb nodded. He understood where Jake was coming from. Jake had had a youthful marriage that only lasted seven months. "Yeah, I know how you feel," he said, "but weddings are important to women, and Marilyn hasn't been married before."

"I know." Jake sighed and ran his hands through his sandy hair. "So I guess I'll go along with her. What the hell. I want her to be happy." His hazel eyes met Caleb's. "Will you be my best man?"

Caleb felt flattered and ridiculously pleased by Jake's request. He reached over and slapped his friend on the back. "I'd be honored. When's the happy event going to take place?"

"The first Saturday in December." Jake shook his head, looking dazed but happy. "Now that I've committed myself, I'd get married next weekend, but Marilyn says it's going to take a few months to make all the arrangements."

"Well, you can count on me to be there to hold you up." They both laughed, then said goodbye.

All the way home Caleb thought about Jake and Marilyn and their coming wedding. For some reason, he felt almost envious of Jake, which was ridiculous because Caleb had no desire to be married. It wasn't that he had anything against the institution, he just didn't think he was cut out for it. But he couldn't help wondering what it would be like to feel so strongly about someone that you wanted to spend the rest of your life with them.

And then, for some reason, Margaret's face floated through his mind.

He shook his head to clear it, telling himself not to romanticize his feelings about Margaret.

You want to make love to her. That's all.

He was still telling himself that at six forty-five when he left to go pick her up.

Margaret took several deep breaths when the doorbell rang promptly at seven o'clock. She glanced at herself in the little mirror gracing the foyer wall as she headed toward the door.

As Caleb had instructed, she'd dressed casually, in a soft white cotton peasant blouse and multicolored full skirt in bright colors. Gold strappy sandals and big gold hoop earrings completed her costume. She'd even curled her hair to enhance the gypsy effect she was striving for. A sharp pang of doubt stabbed her. Was this look too young for her? Did she look ridiculous in this getup? Should she hurry and change into something more conservative?

Then she thought, oh, who cared? This would be the last time she'd see Caleb, so what he thought didn't matter. Besides, it was too late to change.

She wet her lips nervously and took a deep breath, then opened the door.

Happiness coursed through her as Caleb's eyes lit up in undisguised admiration. "Don't you look nice," he said softly, smiling down at her.

"Thank you." Nice was too innocuous a word to describe his appearance, she thought, taking in the way his open-necked blue shirt complemented the deep blue of his eyes and the pulse-accelerating way his jeans hugged his legs and thighs.

"Ready to go?" he asked, stepping inside.

"Yes." She reached for her shoulder bag sitting on the small mahogany table to one side of the foyer.

He glanced around. "This is a beautiful place."

"Thank you. It's kind of big for one person, but it was a nice place to raise the kids."

He smiled at her again, and something about his expression caused that half-scary, half-delicious shivery sensation in the pit of her stomach—the same one she'd had on Saturday when he'd said he wanted to kiss her.

Calm down, Margaret, she told herself as they walked outside. Remember, you're going to stick to your resolve. This is the last time you're going to see him.

As they approached the small red convertible sitting in her driveway, he said, "I told you I had a car." With a flourish, he opened the passenger door.

Margaret chuckled. "This is a car? Looks more like a jelly bean to me."

"You're just saying that because it's true."

Margaret laughed.

"In fact," he said, "that's what my sister Kathleen said when she saw it for the first time."

By now he'd gotten into the car. He started it and backed out of the driveway, flashing her a devilish grin in the process.

Margaret decided he had the most captivating smile she'd ever seen. "Somehow I expected you to have a convertible," she said, wondering if all men had a thing about sports cars. Anthony had bought himself a black

Porsche on his fortieth birthday. Margaret had just sold the car two months ago. And Tony, her son, had recently gifted himself with a white Corvette. Even Keith, Lisa's husband, as shy and quiet as he was, drove one of those new little Hondas similar to this car of Caleb's. Perhaps, Margaret thought, buying yourself a sports car was a rite of passage, a symbol of manhood.

Or perhaps, she thought as Caleb expertly shifted gears and roared off down the street, they were simply fun to drive. She waved at Betty Flack, a neighbor who was out in front of her home moving her sprinkler. Even though Margaret didn't really want to call attention to herself, she knew it would have been far worse to ignore Betty, who had stared openmouthed as they drove past. Especially since Margaret wasn't exactly inconspicuous in this bright little convertible.

Margaret wondered how many other people would see and recognize her before she reached the safety of Caleb's home. "Where do you live?" she asked.

"On Revere Street."

"Really?" She wondered how Caleb could afford a home in that location. Revere Street was one of four original streets laid out when the town was built, and it contained many of the oldest and stateliest homes in the city. They were also the most expensive, even surpassing costly new neighborhoods like hers.

It didn't take them long to get there, for which Margaret was extremely grateful. The fewer people who saw her with him, the better. As he drove down the broad, tree-lined street, she wondered which home belonged to him. When he turned into the driveway of the Cameron house, she was delighted to discover he was living in the carriage house located at the rear of their property. She'd always been fascinated by the few carriage houses still remaining in the area and had often wished Anthony was the type of person to appreciate the older properties of Riverview.

"Here we are," he announced, driving around to the back of the house and parking his car under a carport that was hidden from the street.

"Aren't you lucky to be living here," Margaret exclaimed as he came around to open her door. "This is a beautiful place."

"Yes, I think so, too. Have you ever been inside a carriage house?"

Margaret shook her head, noticing that all the windows were open. "No air conditioning?"

He opened the back door and stood aside to let her precede him. "I've got a window unit in the bedroom, but I rarely use it."

The interior of the house was much cooler than Margaret would have expected. She guessed it was because the carriage house was all brick and shaded by enormous old elm trees. They were in the kitchen, and she noticed that Caleb had a window fan turned on. Delicious smells emanated from a pot on the stove, and Margaret sniffed. "Something smells awfully good."

Caleb grinned. "I hope it is. It's my own recipe."

When he didn't elaborate, Margaret decided she could wait to find out what they were going to eat. She looked around the kitchen, liking the simplicity of it. The floor was a cool, dark stone tile in a shade of slate blue, and the walls were painted white. White curtains hung at the windows, and the countertops were devoid of clutter, although there were several healthy-looking plants in clay pots dotting the surfaces.

A small round white table graced the center of the room, circled by four chairs.

"Come on," Caleb said, "let's get you settled in the living room, then I'll get you something cool to drink."

"Okay." Margaret followed him through the kitchen, down a short hallway, then into the living room, which ran across the front of the house. The same dark tile covered the floor, but an oriental rug in rich jewel tones softened and warmed the room. The furniture was simple and masculine: a burgundy leather sectional sofa, oak coffee table and side tables, an entertainment center containing CD player, VCR and TV set, a bookcase crammed to overflowing, a small walnut desk and chair, and Caleb's fiddle case propped in one corner. The setting sun gilded the furniture and floor, and the filmy curtains fluttered in the breeze generated by another large window fan. Margaret thought how masculine the room looked, just like its owner.

"It's simple, but I like it," Caleb said, giving her another of his heart-stopping smiles.

Margaret sat on one end of the couch. "I like it, too. The furniture's yours, isn't it?"

"Yes."

"For some reason I had the idea this place came furnished."

"It did, but the Camerons generously offered to store most of what was here. The only things that belong to them are the carpet and that little desk."

"How long have you lived here?"

"About eight years."

"Is that how long you've taught at the university?"

"No. For the first two years, I lived in the Riverview Apartments, but then I heard about this house, and I snapped it up. I hate apartments, maybe because we lived in such cramped quarters when I was a kid." He smiled. "Now...what would you like to drink? I've got some chardonnay, or I could fix you a mixed drink of some kind. Or else there's iced tea."

"Chardonnay sounds nice." Margaret thought that she'd had more alcohol to drink in the past couple of days than she'd had in the past couple of months.

"Help yourself to some cheese and crackers," he said, pointing to a glass serving plate on the coffee table.

He disappeared into the kitchen, and Margaret stood and walked over to the bookcase. In her experience, you could tell a lot about a person by the books they read.

Caleb's bookcase was stuffed with the classics, which Margaret had expected given his profession, but it was the modern stuff that interested her. She smiled and decided that in this area, too, he showed what she considered a typical male preference: Elmore Leonard, Robert Ludlum, Robert B. Parker and John Grisham. But she also noticed several novels by Anne Rice and a couple of intriguing non-fiction titles—one a thick history of Ireland and another about global warming.

She was reminded of Floyd Hubbard's tirade the previous evening and made a mental note to ask Caleb if he was involved in the airport controversy.

"Do you like to read?"

Margaret turned. Caleb stood a few feet away, a glass of wine in each hand. She took the glass he held out to her and replied, "Yes, I love to read. I always have, ever since I was a kid." She chuckled. "I was one of those kids who read by flashlight under the covers when my mother thought I was asleep." Then she grimaced, remembering how coldly disapproving her mother would be whenever Margaret got caught. Margaret had never been able to understand why her mother took Margaret's minor rebellion as a personal affront instead of the perfectly natural kind of thing that kids do. When she met Caleb's gaze, his blue eyes were quizzical.

"What were you thinking just now?" he said.

She shrugged. "Oh, nothing important."

Before sitting down he turned on one of the lamps, which cast a soft golden glow on the darkening room. Then he sat on the other end of the couch from her, leaned back and propped one leg across the other. "It was important enough to make you look sad."

Margaret sipped at her wine. "I was thinking about my mother. How she always got angry over such little things." She met his gaze, thinking what sympathetic, warm eyes he had. The kind of eyes that made you want to tell him everything. "Was your mother like that?"

"Nope. My mother's the type who doesn't get upset about anything. Good thing, too. Living on top of each other the way we did, we were always arguing or fighting about something." He grinned, and Margaret saw the affection in his eyes. "The Mahoneys are a noisy, passionate bunch."

Noisy. Passionate.

Margaret couldn't imagine anyone describing the Guthries as noisy or passionate. In fact, more than once she'd wondered how her cold mother and her reserved father had ever managed to produce two children.

In her wildest imaginings, she couldn't picture her mother acting or feeling the way Margaret had acted and felt the other day when Caleb had kissed her. As soon as the thought crossed Margaret's mind, she tried to suppress it. She would become flustered and nervous again if she allowed herself to think about her attraction to Caleb. "Your mother sounds like someone I'd like," she said. "Does she ever come to visit you?"

"Not often. I usually go down to the city. It's easier that way because I can see everyone at the same time."

"Do all of your family live in the city?"

"All but one brother who moved to Boston."

"I love New York," Margaret said. "Wouldn't want to live there, of course, but it's a great place to visit."

Caleb met her gaze. "Actually," he said slowly, "I'm thinking of moving back there in January."

Chapter Seven

Margaret suddenly understood what people meant when they said their hearts sank. Hers hit bottom at the notion that Caleb might leave Riverview in just a few short months. "Oh...I—I'm sorry to hear that."

His eyes held hers. "It's not final or anything. I'm just mulling over the idea right now."

Margaret had regained her equilibrium and her voice felt steadier as she answered. "What would you do if you moved?"

"I've had an offer from Columbia University. They'll have an opening in January, and it's mine if I want it."

"Oh," Margaret said again. Columbia University would be a real step up from a small liberal arts college like Riverview. She swallowed and tried to ignore the lump of disappointment that had settled into her chest. *Why are you disappointed? You weren't planning to see him again, anyway, right?* "That sounds wonderful," she said, forcing enthusiasm into her voice.

Caleb nodded, his blue eyes thoughtful. "It is, in lots of ways, but there are reasons why I'd hate to leave here, too."

"I know why I'd hate to leave Riverview, but I'm curious about your reasons." Margaret sipped at her wine again. She was pleased that she'd managed to sound casual, to inject a note of this-conversation-isn't-important-it's-just-interesting into her response.

"Well, in the first place, I've got tenure here." He grinned. "Of course, tenure has never meant much to me."

"I thought tenure was what all teachers strive for."

He shrugged. "I don't know. I don't like the feeling of being tied down." His eyes twinkled. "It's the rebel in me."

Yes, she could see that. She had instinctively known that he would chafe at rules and restrictions. "What are your other reasons?" she asked, deciding it would be safer not to pursue the rebel comment.

"Friends. And Riverview's a nice place to live." He toyed with his wineglass. "But New York's got a lot going for it."

Margaret knew, for her own peace of mind, it would be immensely better for Caleb to be hundreds of miles away. But she still couldn't completely banish the empty feeling the thought of his leaving had created, and she knew then that no matter how determined she had been to stop seeing him, a part of her had not been reconciled to her decision.

Caleb eyed her wineglass, which was about two-thirds empty. "More wine?"

Margaret shook her head. "I'm fine, thanks." She smiled. "So, are you leaning toward accepting the offer?"

"I don't know. Depends."

Suddenly his eyes seemed darker than they had before as they met hers. Margaret wet her lips. "On what?" She raised her glass to her mouth and took another sip to have something to do, something to dispel the butterflies that had begun to flutter in her stomach.

His eyes never left hers. "Some of it depends on you."

Margaret's heart gave a giant leap, and she nearly choked on the wine. She felt trapped by emotions beyond her control as Caleb set his wineglass down, slowly stood and walked the few feet separating them. She looked up as he reached for her hand and slowly pulled her to a standing position. When he took her wineglass out of suddenly nerveless fingers, she felt completely incapable of resisting him.

She knew she should say something. She knew that if she told him not to, he would back off, but she didn't want him to back off.

She wanted him to kiss her.

She wanted him to put his hands on her shoulders and push her peasant blouse down. She wanted him to touch her and make her feel the way she'd felt on Saturday. Then she wanted him to make love to her. She wanted to feel those strong, slow hands move over her skin. She wanted to feel that urgency and fire, those deliciously wonderful sensations he had kindled the other day, and this time she wanted them to burst into full flame, to reach the intensity she knew they could reach.

She had lied to herself.

She had known all along that this is what she'd come here for tonight.

Why else had she worn her filmiest and laciest underwear?

Why else had she taken such care with her body, showering slowly, rubbing scented cream into her skin, perfuming herself everywhere?

Why else had she worn clothing that would easily slide off with no zippers or hindrances of any kind to impede Caleb's access to her?

This is what you wanted, Margaret.

This is what you wanted all along.

Caleb had intended to feed her, to play soft music, to woo her. He had intended to wait until later before initiating anything intimate, but when she'd looked at him that way, with undisguised and naked longing in those huge eyes with their golden lights, he'd felt such need, such passion and tenderness and urgency, he was powerless to stop himself.

Now, as he slowly gathered her into his arms and lowered his head to kiss her, he knew this moment had been inevitable.

And he could also tell, from her immediate response, the way she opened her mouth to his and wound her soft arms around him, that she knew it, too.

He closed his eyes and gave himself up to the torrent of emotions and sensations pouring through him.

He tasted the tangy residue of wine on her tongue, mingled with the hot sweetness of her breath, and his blood pounded through his veins as the kiss deepened. He burrowed the fingers of his right hand into the silky texture of her hair while his left stroked her back through the soft cotton of her blouse.

Slow, slow, he told himself. Go slow. This is special. Don't rush it. Don't rush her.

He purposely gentled the kiss, then whispered against her open mouth. "Do you want this, Meggy? If not, say so now." Although he knew he shouldn't, knew it was unfair, he slowly moved his hands around to brush the sides of her breasts, feeling their richness and promise. He wanted her so badly at this moment he didn't know how he would stand it if she told him no. But this had to be her decision. He would never force her.

She trembled, and one hand shakily touched his cheek. "Yes, I want this," she whispered back.

With a low cry, Caleb crushed her to him again, kissing her fully and deeply. Then, before things careened out of his control, he lifted her in his arms and carried her into his bedroom.

Margaret closed her eyes and didn't open them again until Caleb gently set her down. They were standing close together in his bedroom, she saw in the dusky light. In the few moments before he slipped his arms around her to kiss her again, Margaret took in the opened windows, the large bed covered with a checkerboard quilt, a chest, a dresser and a nightstand with a lamp and a telephone on top.

And then Caleb's mouth claimed hers, and Margaret forgot about her surroundings, forgot about her misgivings, forgot about her resolutions, and there was only Caleb.

Caleb.

She breathed him in. She absorbed him. She closed her eyes once more and let her feelings take over.

She felt his tongue as it slipped into her mouth.

She felt its heat, its strength, as it touched hers, then delved deeper.

She felt his hands as they made a slow, slow foray into her hair.

She felt the strength and firmness of his chest as he pulled her closer.

She felt the tingling awareness of her breasts and belly and all her more intimate parts as his hands trailed tenderly and knowingly across her bare back, down, down, until they rested against her rump. She could feel their heat as they gently but firmly pulled her closer.

He didn't crush her. There was no roughness to his touch. Only the gentlest brushing of fingers and palms as he stroked her and kissed her.

Margaret's heart beat in slow, heavy thuds that quickened as the seconds ticked on. She placed her palms against his chest, and felt his heart echoing hers.

She felt as if her body had been sapped of its will, drained of its strength, as she melted under Caleb's touch.

His mouth dropped to her neck, her shoulders, and then, just as she'd wanted him to, his hands slowly pulled the elastic neckline of her blouse over and down her shoulders, exposing more of her to his mouth and fingertips.

As each inch of skin was bared, he kissed it, running his tongue lovingly over its surface. Margaret shivered as he finally slipped her blouse all the way down and helped her free her arms. Then, eyes gleaming in the twilight, he touched her through the satin and lace of her bra. He smiled, his breathing accelerating, as she moaned.

She reached up, intending to unhook her bra.

"No," he said, his voice ragged. "Not yet."

He unbuttoned his shirt, his eyes never leaving her face, and all Margaret could hear was their quickened breathing, all she could feel was the fire in her veins, the need pounding inside her.

He threw his shirt on the floor, then, making a visible effort to control his own urgency, he slowly drew her forward again. Hands cupping her breasts, he kissed her mouth, her eyes, her cheeks, then trailed down her neck to the exposed tops of her breasts. He pushed her breasts up, and Margaret whimpered as his tongue moved over the satin of her bra to find an aching crest. There was something so incredibly erotic about the feel of his tongue against the wet satin. And when his teeth gently nipped, Margaret gasped.

She hardly realized that he had pushed her blouse and skirt down until she felt them slide to the floor. All she could concentrate on was the heat and pull of his mouth and tongue on her aching breasts.

When he finally unhooked her bra and drew her against him so that bare skin touched bare skin, Margaret was shaking. He held her for a long moment, then whispered, "Let's get rid of the rest of these clothes, okay?"

Margaret nodded.

Within moments, his jeans and briefs hit the floor, then he helped her roll her panties down. If there had been more light in the room, Margaret knew she would have been scared, because hers was not a young body, even though she'd always taken care of it and was secretly proud of her success in keeping it supple and looking good. But the light was very dim, and Caleb didn't give her time to think.

Again he lifted her, and this time he set her gently on the bed, then lay down beside her, turning to face her. Wordlessly he kissed her and began to touch her again.

All Margaret's secret fantasies about a slow-handed lover burst into life, and the reality was even better than her dreams.

His hands were like velvet as they whispered over her body. Margaret floated in sensation, feeling like a flower blooming in the sunshine as radiance spread through her. Slowly, so very slowly, Caleb's hands became more insistent, more demanding, and Margaret, feeling a corresponding urgency throbbing deep inside, got brave enough to touch Caleb, too.

He sucked in his breath as her fingertips brushed over his chest. He felt so different from Anthony, Margaret discovered, and she loved the differences, as she'd known she would. It wasn't just that Caleb was younger, his flesh firmer, his body more resilient. The differences were more subtle, more to do with responses and reactions.

Margaret closed her eyes and pushed the thoughts of Anthony from her mind. This was her time. She didn't want it spoiled by memory or guilt or anything remotely connected. This might be the only time she and Caleb ever made love, and she wanted to savor each moment so that years from now, when she was an old woman, she could take out this memory and relive it, again and again.

"Beautiful Meggy," he murmured. He kissed her ear. "I hate to bring this up, but do I need to use—"

"No," Margaret said, cutting him off. "It's okay." She'd had her tubes tied after Lori was born, so there was no chance of a pregnancy.

"Good," he said, his lips feathering her cheek, her neck, her breasts, then moving lower. She tensed only once, when she felt his mouth on her belly. She wished so much that she were younger, firmer, more beautiful. She knew he probably couldn't help but compare her to other women, and she was so afraid he would find her lacking.

When he turned her slowly, she didn't resist. Nothing *he* did frightened her. It was only her own inadequacies that scared her. She knew instinctively that Caleb would never hurt her.

He settled her up against him, her back to his chest. He lifted her right leg and placed it over his, and Margaret let him, opening herself willingly.

Against her bottom she could feel the heat of his erection pushing against her, and she shivered and nestled closer. Caleb's hands tightened around her, then began their slow journey of exploration once more.

Margaret moaned as he caressed her ever more insistently. And when one hand clamped over her breasts, rubbing the tight, aching buds, and the other moved down to probe until his fingers slipped inside and found her pulsing core, she whimpered.

"Shh," he said, kissing her ear as his fingers began to move in slow circles. Within only seconds, Margaret arched, unable to stop or even slow down the shattering climax that tore a cry from her lips. It rushed through her in wave after wave, an exquisite torment that Caleb wouldn't allow her to escape, even if she'd wanted to. He held her until her body stopped its shuddering, until she lay limp and damp and spent.

Then, and only then, did he turn her onto her back, part her legs and slowly enter her.

He pushed deep inside, and Margaret welcomed him, wrapping her legs around him, feeling the steel and heat as it filled her. When he began to move, she moved with him, and slowly, they found their own, unique rhythm.

Margaret had never had more than one orgasm during lovemaking. Many times she hadn't even had one. More times than she wanted to remember, she had only pretended.

Tonight she knew she would have another. The sensations quickly began to build again, the delicious tension, the almost unbearable anticipation, that feeling that she was perched on the edge of a very high cliff, and in only moments, would plunge in a wild freefall.

Sure enough, as Caleb's thrusts became harder, Margaret could feel her body tensing in preparation, and within moments, she catapulted over the edge. Almost simultaneously, Caleb gave a great shudder and spasms racked his sweat-slicked body and she felt him spilling into her.

When he was spent, he collapsed against her, and Margaret held him tight, held him until his body calmed, and their hearts slowed. When he would have moved, she wouldn't let him.

"Stay here," she whispered. "Stay inside me." Anthony had never stayed inside her when he'd reached his climax. He had pulled out, given her a perfunctory kiss on the cheek, said, "Good night, Margaret," and rolled over and gone immediately to sleep.

Margaret had lain there listening to him snore.

So she held Caleb prisoner and reveled in the feeling of power it gave her.

Caleb buried his face in her neck and stayed where he was.

Margaret felt whole in a way she'd never felt whole before. She knew it was corny, but she felt as if she'd come home after a long absence.

Oh, Caleb, her heart cried. *What have you done to me?*

She wished she could stay here, just like this, forever. She wished she didn't have to move, didn't have to think, didn't have to talk, didn't have to face tomorrow.

Everything in her universe, everything familiar, had changed irrevocably.

Especially her.

She knew that nothing would ever look the same again. She knew she would never view the world or anyone in it in quite the same way.

She was more frightened than she'd ever been in her entire life.

Chapter Eight

For the next twenty-four hours, Caleb walked around in a daze. He wasn't sure exactly what had happened to him, but from the moment he began making love to Margaret, he had been a changed man.

He felt stunned.

That was the only word that fitted.

Stunned.

As in bamboozled, shocked, speechless, paralyzed, astonished and completely flabbergasted.

Not to mention confused.

He felt as if someone had hit him over the head with a hammer. He couldn't think straight.

What was wrong with him? he asked himself Tuesday morning as he tried to concentrate on his lecture. When he'd stumbled and lost his place for the fourth time in fifteen minutes, he gave a self-deprecating laugh, looked up at the semicircle of students in the lecture hall and said, "I'm feeling a little groggy today. How about if I let you guys go early?"

There was a rush of bodies and a few cheers as the students made good their escape, probably afraid he might change his mind.

Caleb gathered his notes and walked slowly back to his office. He sank behind his desk and propped his feet up on top of it. He stared at the wall.

Margaret.

Closing his eyes, he let her image invade his mind. Lord, but she was sweet. Making love to her had been incredible. Not that she was a very skillful lover, he thought ruefully. In fact, she seemed to know awfully little about making love, although she'd certainly been game to learn. Caleb smiled, thinking about the way they'd teased each other during dinner and then later, how responsive and willing she'd been when they'd gone back to bed.

But Margaret's skill or lack of it had nothing to do with Caleb's feelings. It was Margaret herself. Her complete acceptance of him and the joy of her response.

For the first time in his life Caleb had felt completely protective of a woman, completely selfless in his lovemaking.

He had wanted her to be happy. He had wanted to give her the greatest possible pleasure, to show her that she was very special to him.

And in the process of this giving, he had received something wonderful himself.

He let his thoughts drift back to the aftermath of their lovemaking the previous evening. He had held her for a long time and she'd been so quiet he'd gotten worried.

"You're not sorry, are you?" he'd finally whispered.

Her arms tightened around him. "No. I'll never be sorry, no matter what happens."

He smiled and stroked her hair. "Good."

"*Y-you're* not sorry, are you?" she asked.

"God, no," he said fiercely. "How could you possibly think I might be?"

"I—I just thought because you asked if I was, maybe you were..." Her voice trailed off uncertainly.

He kissed her, letting his lips linger against the warmth of hers as he murmured, "The only reason I asked if you were sorry is because you were so quiet. I was afraid you might be having second thoughts." He kissed her again, then stroked her cheek. "Tonight was wonderful. One of the best things that's ever happened to me. *You're* one of the best things that's ever happened to me."

"Caleb, you don't have to say things like that."

"What do you mean?" he asked, honestly confused.

"I just mean, well, you don't have to try to make me feel good."

"Make you feel good! Is that what you think I'm doing?" He released her and rolled over to turn on the bedside lamp so he could see her face. When he did, she curled into herself, as if she were ashamed to have him see her naked.

"Margaret," he said gently, filled with an emotion he couldn't identify. He reached for her, drawing her close again. He kissed her cheek and stroked her back until he felt her relax in his arms. "I was being honest about my feelings. When you know me better, you'll know I don't say things I don't mean. Now, will you please tell me why you tried to cover yourself?''

She buried her face against his chest, and her words were muffled as she answered. ''I—I...oh, Caleb, you've been with young, beautiful women. I'm not... I'm—''

''Shh,'' he said. ''Don't say another word. *You* are a young, beautiful woman. And you're the only woman I want. What do I have to do to prove it to you?''

She didn't answer, just lifted her face to gaze into his eyes. After a long moment, she pulled his head down, and Caleb forgot everything but the woman in his arms and the powerful feelings raging through him.

And now, as he once more relived last night, his body responded with a storm of emotions that rocked him with their intensity, and Caleb knew his life had changed irrevocably.

''Hellooo! Margaret? Is anybody home?'' The sing-song voice was accompanied by a loud rattling of the screen door.

Margaret wrapped a towel around her wet head and hurried downstairs. She saw Betty Flack's dyed platinum head through the screen. It was Tuesday afternoon, and Margaret had a feeling she knew exactly why Betty had come calling.

''Hi, Betty,'' she said as she opened the door. ''Come on in.''

Betty, short and plump, wore a brightly flowered sun suit and big-brimmed gardening hat. In her hand was a basket of fat red tomatoes. ''Brought you some of my tomatoes. Got too many for just us. Thought you could probably put 'em to use.''

"Why, thanks," Margaret said. She secured the towel more firmly and took the tomatoes. "That was nice of you." She smiled.

For a moment, there was an awkward silence. Margaret knew Betty expected her to invite her into the living room, to offer her a cold drink. Margaret also knew that if she did, she would be subjected to questions she'd rather not have to answer. She was positive Betty had not come over solely to give her tomatoes.

While Margaret was still trying to decide what to do, Betty said, "Have you got a minute? I wanted to talk to you about Punky's fiftieth birthday party."

Punky was Betty's husband, and Margaret wasn't sure how or why the swarthy man who looked as if he were an ex-prize fighter had ever been dubbed with the name. Anthony, in a typical put-down of anyone different from him, had once said Punky Flack had probably come by the name honestly. "He looks like he was a street punk when he was young," Anthony had sneered.

"Well, my hair's wet..." Margaret said, pushing away the remembrance of Anthony's unkind remark.

"I'll only keep you a few minutes," Betty said.

"I guess I've got a few minutes before I have to get ready to leave." Margaret motioned to the living room. "Why don't you go on in and have a seat? Can I bring you something to drink?"

"Ice tea would be nice," Betty said.

Although Margaret hadn't intended to go out until her job tonight—catering a baby shower at the country club—she decided she hadn't really lied to Betty. She actually needed a few things at the supermarket, and once her neighbor had left, Margaret would go get them.

When Margaret returned to the living room with Betty's glass of tea, she saw the woman had settled herself into one of the yellow-and-white striped satin Queen Anne chairs that flanked Margaret's fireplace.

Margaret sat in its twin and said, "So when is Punky's birthday?"

For the next ten minutes Betty explained what she wanted to do for her husband's party. She finished with, "And the most important thing is it must be a surprise, Margaret. That's mainly why I want you to do everything. That way Punky won't suspect a thing!"

"I'll be happy to take care of it. I'll write the date down just as soon as I go back upstairs to my office." Margaret hoped Betty would take her gentle hint and say goodbye.

But Betty settled deeper into her chair. She cocked her head and smiled at Margaret. "I'm glad things are working out for you," she said. Although her eyes were speculative, her smile seemed genuine. "I have to admit, though, I was a little shocked when I saw you with that young man last night." She watched Margaret carefully.

Margaret's stomach tightened. She reminded herself that she really did like Betty, that the woman's curiosity was only normal. But why did everyone persist in calling Caleb a *young* man? Was there no other adjective that came to mind when people looked at him?

Face it, Margaret. He is young. As a matter of fact, he's eight years younger than you are. "Why were you shocked?" she managed to say in a more or less normal voice.

"Well, maybe shocked is too strong a word. I guess I was just surprised. I didn't realize you were dating anyone yet. Although there's nothing *wrong* with that," she hastened to add.

"I'm really not *dating*," Margaret said quickly. Too quickly, she realized immediately.

"Oh? Well, I guess I just assumed..."

"Caleb's just a friend. He...uh...took me to dinner." *Boy, lying is getting to be a bad habit, Margaret.*

Betty just looked at her. Margaret could almost see the wheels turning in her head. *Just a friend. He...uh...took me to dinner.* Even to Margaret's ears, her words sounded inane and evasive.

She abruptly stood and looked at her watch again. "Listen, Betty," she said, desperation edging her voice, "I really do have to get ready. I have a job tonight." That wasn't another lie, Margaret assured herself.

Not really.

Betty looked as if she'd like to say more. Ask more. But she stood, too.

Relief flooded Margaret as she led the way to the front door. Only a few more minutes and Betty would be gone.

Just as Betty opened the screen door to walk outside, a white paneled truck turned into Margaret's driveway. Margaret stared. Bouquets By Brenda was emblazoned on the side in bright pink letters.

"Looks like you're getting some flowers," Betty said, giving Margaret a thoughtful look. "Is it your birthday or something?"

"No," Margaret said, her mouth dry. "It's not my birthday." Who was sending her flowers? She swallowed. Caleb. Of course.

The driver hopped out of the truck, slid open the side panel, and extracted a long white box tied with a red satin ribbon. He cut across the lawn, spotted Margaret and Betty in the doorway and smiled, saying, "Ms. Desmond?" He looked from one to the other.

Margaret cleared her throat. "I'm Margaret Desmond." She even managed to smile.

The boy thrust the box into her hands, said, "Have a nice day," and strode back to the truck. Seconds later it disappeared down the street.

"Well, aren't you going to open the card?" Betty said.

Margaret blinked. She had almost forgotten Betty was still there. "Uh, no," she stammered. "N-not this minute. I have to go dry my hair."

Only after Betty, who very obviously didn't want to, had gone, did Margaret realize how incredibly stupid she must have sounded.

Closing the screen door and latching it, Margaret walked into the living room, sat on the edge of the sofa, and stared at the box. With fingers that trembled, she broke the seal on the envelope attached to the red ribbon and removed the small card.

"I'll never forget last night."

She took a deep, shaky breath as she stared at the bold scrawl. Her first thought was, *I'll never forget last night, either.* Her second thought was, *Oh, God, Brenda Luce probably took this order.* Brenda Luce was just about as big a gossip as Phyllis Dixon.

But then Margaret scrutinized the note more carefully. This handwriting looked like the handwriting on the note that had accompanied the picnic basket. Relief flooded her. Caleb had written the note himself. Brenda hadn't seen it. Margaret thanked God fervently, even as the impact of Caleb's words settled into her brain.

I'll never forget last night.

Last night.

All day Margaret had thought of little else. She had relived, over and over again, the things she and Caleb had done and said and all the things she had felt. She'd walked around in a fog, unable to shut off the images.

She'd been alternately wildly happy and indescribably sad. Sometimes she could feel herself blushing. Sometimes she couldn't believe any of it had actually happened, but then all she'd had to do was feel the unaccustomed sensitivity of certain parts of her body, and she knew last night hadn't been a dream.

Oh, no, it had been deliciously real.

Wonderfully, incredibly real.

Unbelievably real.

The realest thing she'd ever experienced except for the birth of her children.

All day her emotions had been chaotic.

They still were.

Sighing, she slowly untied the ribbon around the box. She opened the lid. Her breath caught as she parted the green tissue paper.

The roses were the palest pink imaginable. Almost white, with just the faintest blush tipping their edges. Tiny drops of moisture beaded them, shimmering in the sunlight. Margaret gently lifted them out and buried her face in the delicate buds. Their gossamer fragrance felt like a caress as it drifted around her.

I'll never forget last night.

Margaret closed her eyes. Silvery images danced through her mind.

I'll never forget last night.

They hadn't eaten until after midnight. They had lain in bed after making love the second time, not talking much, just holding each other. Once in a while Caleb would kiss her nose or her eyelids, and Margaret would sigh.

For a little while, they slept.

Finally Caleb stirred and said, "I promised you dinner. Why don't we go eat?"

"All right," Margaret said, even though she wasn't the least bit hungry.

They'd gotten up, and Caleb had refused to let her get dressed in her clothes. "Oh, no, sweet Meggy," he said when she reached for her undergarments. He pulled her into his arms and kissed her soundly. Then he laughed and said, "I intend to make love to you again, after we have our dinner." His smile turned wicked. "Clothes would just get in the way."

Margaret blushed at the promise in his eyes.

He pulled dark blue silk pajamas out of his chest of drawers and tossed her the top, which, when she put it on and belted it, just hit the tops of her thighs.

"Yes," he said, eyeing her, "oh, yes," and Margaret blushed again. She felt self-conscious, but she liked the glitter of admiration in his eyes as his gaze swept her legs.

He put on the bottoms, and they rode low on his hips. Margaret thought he looked impossibly sexy. She loved the look of his bare chest, which was mostly smooth and tanned, as if he'd spent hours in the sun. She loved the V of dark curls that disappeared into his waistband. She already knew how springy they felt to her touch. She loved his bare feet, which made him look somehow vulnerable as he stood there laughing at her while she inspected him.

"Do I pass?" he said.

"With flying colors," she answered. Then, completely surprising herself, she said, "I like looking at you."

"Woman," he teased. "If you keep saying things like that, I might forget all about dinner."

Margaret surprised herself again by answering, "That would be fine with me."

They'd eaten their dinner in the kitchen, and Margaret was glad it was at the back of the house and no one from the street could see them through the open windows. She could just imagine what kinds of comments she'd have to contend with if anyone should spy her dressed the way she was dressed. When the thought formed, she tried to banish it. Right then she didn't want to think about consequences. All she wanted to think about was Caleb.

All through dinner, Caleb made outrageously suggestive remarks about what they would do later. At first, Margaret was embarrassed and shy. Then she realized it was a game, so, shrugging off her inhibitions, she entered into the spirit of it.

When he said, "I don't intend to let you get any sleep tonight," she said, "Anyone can talk big. It's performance that counts."

When he said, "Maybe we should try position number twelve, what do you think?" she said, "Hmm. Position number twelve? I don't know. Are you sure you're up for it?"

Then she'd dissolved into giggles when he pulled the elastic of his pajama bottoms out and peered inside.

"Yep," he'd said, looking at her with sparkling eyes, "I'm definitely *up* for it."

Eventually, full of good food and a nice, keen edge of anticipation, they went back to Caleb's bed and he made good on all his promises.

But the night had to end sometime. About two-thirty, Margaret sighed and said, "I've got to get home, Caleb."

"Why? Why not just spend the night?" He tweaked her nose. "I'll cook you breakfast in the morning. I make a mean omelet."

She wanted to. The thought of falling asleep in his arms, waking to the smells of breakfast and the sight of Caleb, was tempting. But she hadn't taken complete leave of her senses. She shook her head regretfully. "Caleb, try to understand, okay? I'm a mother of grown children, and a fairly recent widow. If I were to spend the night, and someone were to see me returning home after the sun came up, people would talk."

"So what? Let them. What we do is our business, no one else's."

Margaret could hear the honest confusion in his voice. She knew for someone like Caleb, her fears probably seemed ridiculous. "That's true, but still . . . I grew up here. And my family is pretty straitlaced. It's bad enough I'm doing something I know they'd disapprove of, but I just don't think I should rub their noses in it."

"Do *you* think we've done something wrong?" Caleb asked quietly.

"No," she hastened to assure him. "No, I don't. But I *do* have to live here."

He nodded, but Margaret wondered if he'd understood at all. It was obvious he cared nothing for other people's opinions. Besides, there was definitely a double standard at work in a situation like this. Caleb could afford to have a casual attitude about having a woman spend the night. He not only had nothing to lose, but he was a man. Men were expected to do this kind of thing. A woman like Margaret was not. She would be talked about; he would receive knowing smiles.

She worried all the way home that one of her neighbors might still be awake, might notice the car and realize it was Margaret. It was with relief that she saw all the houses on her street were dark and shuttered for the night.

When Caleb drew her into his arms for a good-night kiss, she was glad she hadn't turned on the outside light before she left the house, glad the shadows surrounded them, even as she reveled in her newfound happiness.

"Think of me tonight, Meggy," he whispered just before he left her. "I'll call you tomorrow."

She had thought of little else.

She'd also worried a little about whether he really would call her.

But now, breathing in the sweetness of the roses, seeing the words he'd written, she knew he would.

When the phone rang about an hour later, she felt a rush of anticipation as she lifted the receiver.

"Margaret?" her mother's voice said.

Oh, no! How had her mother found out about last night so soon? "Hello, Mother," Margaret said, resignation settling like a heavy lump in her chest.

"What's the matter?"

"Nothing. Did I sound like something's the matter?"

"Well, you certainly didn't sound like yourself."

"I had a frog in my throat." Margaret cleared her throat for emphasis.

"Are you busy?" her mother said.

"Not real busy. I was just getting ready to make out a shopping list." Maybe her mother *hadn't* heard about last night.

"Have you talked to Lori since school started?"

"No. She hasn't called."

"And you haven't called her?"

Margaret sighed. "No, Mother. I promised myself I wouldn't hover over her. She'll call me if she needs anything."

"I still think—"

"If you're worried about her, why don't *you* call her?"

"You don't have to take that tone with me, Margaret."

Margaret counted to ten. "I'm sorry. I just, well, you know how things are between me and Lori. I don't want to make them worse, and if she thinks I'm checking up on her, she'll get mad."

"Yes, I know, dear," Joyce said, her voice softening. "I know things have been difficult since dear Anthony passed away."

Margaret let the remark pass, even though she wanted to say things had been difficult even before dear Anthony passed away. But she didn't think her mother would appreciate the sarcasm. Why had her mother called, anyway? Joyce rarely called just to talk. Usually she had a purpose, but so far she'd given Margaret no hint of what it might be.

As if she'd read Margaret's mind, Joyce said, "The reason I called is I thought perhaps you might like to join me for dinner tonight. Marlene put a pot roast on before she left." Marlene was her mother's three-times-a-week housekeeper.

"Oh, Mother, I'd love to, but I can't. I've got a job at the country club tonight."

"Oh. What kind of a job?"

"It's a baby shower for Shelley Siskowic. Her sister Grace and Fran Wagner are giving it."

"Oh, well, that's too bad."

Margaret heard the faint note of disapproval in her mother's voice. Joyce had not been enthusiastic when Margaret started her business. Joyce had made no secret of the fact that she thought if Margaret was determined to work, she should have found a normal daytime job. It irritated Joyce that Margaret was so often busy at night or on the weekends.

"I never see you anymore," Joyce said.

"That's not true. We saw each other Sunday."

"For five minutes, after church."

"I'm sorry. I'll try to stop by later in the week. Maybe we could have lunch together Thursday or Friday."

"Let's set a date now," Joyce said. "Friday's good for me. How about twelve-thirty at the club?"

Margaret grimaced. She hated eating lunch at the country club, but she knew better than to say so. Joyce loved seeing and being seen, and the club was the place to do it. "All right."

After they'd hung up, Margaret sat for a few minutes and thought about the conversation. Obviously her mother had not yet heard about Margaret seeing Caleb the previous evening. If Margaret were very lucky, she might never hear, but the chances were that by Friday, she probably would.

Oh, well, Margaret thought, she'd have to get the confrontation over with sometime. Sighing deeply, wondering why life had to be so complicated, she stood and walked back toward the kitchen. She glanced at the clock. It was five o'clock already, and by six-thirty, she would need to be on her way. If Caleb didn't phone soon, she would miss his call.

She needn't have worried. Barely ten minutes later, the phone rang again, and this time, when she answered it, she heard his low voice on the other end.

"Hello, Meggy," he said.

Margaret's heart beat faster, and there was a little catch in her voice as she said, "Hello, Caleb."

His voice dropped a notch. "God, it's good to hear your voice. I've been thinking about you all day."

Something warm and wonderful filled Margaret's chest. "Me, too."

He laughed softly. "That's good. Did the flowers come?"

"Oh, yes, and they're beautiful, Caleb. Thank you."

"I meant what I said."

I'll never forget last night. She could feel the thought vibrate over the telephone wire. "Caleb," she whispered, "I'll never forget last night, either."

"Meggy?"

"Yes?"

"Am I going to see you again?"

Margaret had wondered what she'd say if he asked her this question. "Do you want to see me again?"

"You know I do."

Margaret closed her eyes. She remembered her promise to herself that last night would be the last time she saw Caleb. *But that was before you made love with him.* "Yes," she finally said. "Yes, I want to see you again."

"How about tonight?"

"Oh, Caleb, I'm sorry, not tonight. I've got a job tonight. I'm catering a baby shower at the country club."

"A baby shower can't last all night, can it?"

"Well, no..."

"What time will you be through?"

Margaret did a quick calculation. "Probably about ten."

"So you should be home by ten-thirty? Eleven?"

"Ten-thirty."

"I'll be waiting for you."

Margaret thought about her neighbors. She thought about her mother. She thought about Phyllis Dixon and others of her ilk. "Okay," she said. "And Caleb?"

"Yes?"

"Pull around back, will you?"

For a moment, there was silence at the other end of the line.

"Meggy," he chided, "you're not ashamed of me, are you?"

"Oh, Caleb, no! But I told you—"

"I know. I know. I'll pull around back. Don't worry."

"It's just that I'd rather avoid talk if I can."

"It's okay, Mrs. Desmond. Believe it or not, I can be circumspect if I have to." He chuckled. "I don't have to like it, though."

Caleb didn't like it at all. He simply couldn't understand why Margaret was so uptight about being seen with him. As he'd pointed out to her, they were both adults, and they were both single.

So why should anyone care what they did?

He guessed, if he and Margaret were going to keep their relationship going for any length of time—and he certainly hoped they would—he'd have to educate her.

Loosen her up.

He grinned. That should be a lot of fun. Margaret seemed to be a quick study; if last night were any indication, broadening her education and perspective ought to be a very enjoyable assignment.

Still . . . he didn't want her to be worried or unhappy, so until she was ready to go public, he'd respect her wishes and try to keep their relationship as low key as possible.

But as he'd told her earlier, he didn't have to like it.

Chapter Nine

Margaret couldn't wait for the baby shower to be over. She hurried through the cleanup, loaded everything into her van and escaped as soon as she could.

She even broke the speed limit on the way home.

Excitement, fear and a delicious sense of the forbidden had her heart thumping like a piston by the time she pulled into her driveway. As instructed, Caleb had pulled his little convertible around the back of the house, where it was parked out of sight of the street.

The lamp mounted over the back door cast enough light to illuminate Caleb, who leaned against his car, legs crossed, a lazy smile on his face. Using the remote, Margaret opened the garage door. By the time she'd parked the van and gotten out, Caleb was walking toward her.

She hit the control to close the garage door, then hurried to meet him.

When Caleb swung her up into his arms, she forgot that she didn't want anyone to see them. She forgot that they were perfectly captured in the golden pool of lamplight. She forgot everything but how much she had wanted to be with him again.

With a glad cry, she wound her arms around his neck and gave herself up to his kiss.

"Meggy, Meggy," he breathed as he finally let her up for air. "I couldn't wait."

"Me, either."

Her entire body strained toward him and he kissed her again, plunging his tongue deep inside as if he couldn't get enough of her fast enough.

This time, when he lifted his head, Margaret said, "Let's go inside."

The moment they were inside the back door, he took her in his arms again. They stood there, in the dark utility room, kissing as if this might be their one and only opportunity.

"I've thought about this all day," he said, his voice rough with desire. He nuzzled her neck and unbuttoned her blouse at the same time. His hands shook a little as they made contact with her skin, and Margaret shivered.

"I know. I did, too." Her breathing was ragged as her hands found the zipper of his jeans.

This time there was no finesse to their lovemaking. No slow hands. No patient preparation and foreplay.

This time they were greedy.

This time they couldn't wait.

This time they made love standing up, with Caleb lifting Margaret and thrusting into her until she cried out.

Afterward, Margaret trembled, and Caleb smoothed her hair back from her face and whispered, "I'm sorry. I didn't hurt you, did I?"

She closed her eyes and held him, feeling his strong heart beating against hers. "No, you didn't hurt me." She reached up, touching her lips to the hollow of his throat. "Come on. Let's go upstairs."

She led him into the guest bedroom, which she'd prepared earlier by closing the blinds, putting fresh sheets on the bed, and lighting a small lamp. Even though she knew, in her head, that there was nothing wrong with them using the master bedroom, she hadn't wanted to. What she'd found with Caleb was too special to mar it with memories of the past.

"I'm sorry the bed's so small," she said, gesturing toward the double bed. "This is a guest bedroom."

He smiled. "It doesn't matter."

As Margaret walked into his arms again, she thought, no, it doesn't matter.

Nothing matters except this.

And at that moment, she really believed it.

The following day Caleb's classes were over at two o'clock, so he and Margaret—who he'd figured would need a lot of persuading but actually needed very little—climbed onto his motorcycle and took off for the countryside.

He didn't know what had caused her change of heart, but after their frenzied lovemaking in her utility room the previous evening, she had done an about-face, and when he'd suggested the excursion on the bike, she'd agreed almost immediately.

"Aren't you worried someone will see you?" he'd asked. Not that he cared, but he didn't want Margaret to be worried the whole time they were gone.

She'd shrugged. "I've decided I'm not going to worry about it anymore. I just want to be with you."

They had a wonderful time riding on the bike. He'd told Margaret to wear jeans to protect her legs and thighs. He thought she looked enchanting in her tennis shoes, tight jeans and red shirt. She'd even tied her hair up with a red ribbon.

"To keep it out of my eyes," she said.

"I love it," he said, brushing his fingers against her neck. "You look like a teenager." She ducked her head shyly, and pink tinged her cheeks.

He loved it when she blushed, loved that a woman her age could still find something to blush about. Most of the women he'd known, some much younger than Margaret, hadn't blushed about anything. They'd been bold and worldly-wise and proud of it. Caleb found it irresistibly appealing that Margaret had this touch of innocence and wonder about her. That the simplest compliment could cause her eyes to light with pleasure and her cheeks to color so becomingly.

They rode for hours, past meadows and ponds, past farms with almost ripened corn and roadside stands loaded with fat peaches, tomatoes and squash. The day was warm, but not unbearably hot, and the sun felt good beating down on their shoulders. About five o'clock, they spotted a dinky little café that sported a couple of picnic tables outside. The tables were covered with blue-and-white checked oilcloths and tin ashtrays and salt and pepper shakers sat like sentries in the middle.

"What do you think?" Caleb said.

"Mom and Pop's," Margaret said, squinting up at the rickety sign swinging in the breeze. "Homemade Burgers." She grinned. "I haven't had a greasy hamburger in years."

Caleb's stomach rumbled. "Okay. This is it."

They ate thick cheeseburgers, oozing with trimmings, and Margaret, eyes shining, nose a little red with sunburn, bemoaned the cholesterol content, but she finished every last drop and even licked her fingers.

Caleb, watching her, felt something twist in his gut and wished the owners of the café weren't quite so in evidence. He wanted to pull Margaret onto his lap and kiss her. He wanted to slide his hand inside her blouse and touch her. He wanted to hear that little catch in her breath as her body responded to him.

Their gazes met across the table, and awareness sizzled in the air between them. Margaret's eyelids drooped, and she took a deep breath. She ran her tongue over her bottom lip, and Caleb nearly moaned with frustration.

"Let's get outta here," he said gruffly.

When they climbed back onto his bike, he could feel every place her body connected with his, and when her palms flattened against his chest, he sucked in his breath.

He turned the bike back in the direction they'd come, and about thirty agonizing minutes later, he found the place he'd remembered—a huge meadow with grass as tall as his waist and no houses nearby.

He pulled the bike into a stand of trees at the edge of the road, jumped off, then helped Margaret down.

Hand in hand, they walked deep into the meadow.

"You know, Caleb," Margaret said, tickling his bare chest with a blade of grass. "This is the very first time

I've ever made love outdoors."

He smiled lazily, and she thought the clear blue of the sky was a perfect backdrop for the wonderful blue of his eyes. "So what'd you think?" he said.

"On a scale of one to ten?"

"Yeah."

Margaret grinned. "Forty!" she said, jumping up. "I'll race you to the bike. Last one there's a lazy slug." She took off as fast as she could, laughing because she could hear Caleb swearing as he tried to get all his clothes back on.

They rode back into Riverview at dusk, and Margaret found herself worrying again, then she got mad at herself. *I want to keep seeing him, so people are going to find out,* she thought. *If I have to put up with some gossip, well, I'll just have to learn to deal with it.* She told herself it would be worth it. It would be worth just about anything to be able to be with Caleb. She had never, not in a million years, imagined she could feel this way about anyone.

She wondered now how she could have ever thought she loved Anthony. What she'd felt for Anthony couldn't compare to what she felt for Caleb.

She couldn't give him up.

She spent the night at his house, but still thought it would be best not to push the limits, so she made him take her home before the sun came up.

On Thursday, Margaret catered a luncheon at one of the stately old homes on Revere Street, only two houses down from where Caleb lived. It gave her a funny feeling to be so close, especially when she knew he had no Thursday afternoon class and was probably at home.

That night, Caleb took her out to dinner. They drove up to Saratoga Springs and ate at an old mill near the racetrack. Margaret got dressed up, wearing a short black crepe dress with cap sleeves and her good pearls, and Caleb wore a dark gray suit and striped tie. Margaret couldn't believe how handsome he looked. He smelled good, too, like crisp mountain air and leafy green forests.

"Wow," she said when she opened her front door.

"Wow, yourself," he said.

The evening seemed magical to Margaret. By the time they reached the restaurant, it was nearly dark, and the air was honey-scented from the sweet alyssum that bordered the entrance. Inside, the candlelight cast flickering shadows across the rough-hewn walls, and Caleb and Margaret sat close together at a small table in the corner.

They ate roasted quail and wild rice and drank a little wine. Then later, after dinner, they danced close together on the small dance floor to the music of a combo that played songs from the 40s.

Caleb seemed to know all the words. "It had to be you," he sang softly.

"Do you do everything well?" Margaret asked.

"What do you mean?"

"Limericks, fiddle playing, singing...dancing."

He chuckled. "You inspire me."

The band segued into "You'll Never Know," and Caleb immediately began to sing along.

"How do you know the words to all these songs?"

"Remember, my mother is a voice teacher."

"Somehow I thought that meant opera."

"Nothing so fancy for Ma. She teaches would-be cabaret singers. That's why she makes so little money."

"So where did you learn to dance like this?" Margaret said as he twirled her around.

He grinned. "I used to date a dancing teacher."

"I should have known."

In answer he pretended to bite her neck.

"Anthony hated to dance," Margaret said when she stopped laughing.

Caleb pulled her closer and murmured in her ear, "Anthony obviously didn't know a good thing when he saw it."

Margaret smiled.

Later, on the way home, Caleb put the top down, and while the balmy night air blew through Margaret's hair and a slow song by Bonnie Raitt played on the radio, Margaret leaned her head on Caleb's shoulder and dreamed of the night ahead.

Much later, feeling languid and sated, Margaret lay in the crook of Caleb's arm and listened to him breathe. "Are you asleep?" she whispered.

His arm tightened around her. "No. Just lying here thinking."

"What are you thinking about?" She drew a lazy circle on his chest.

He didn't answer for a long time. Just as Margaret thought she might ask him again, he turned to face her, cupping her face with his free hand. He kissed her mouth softly, letting his tongue linger against her lips. His eyes were dark pools in the dim room. It was very quiet. The only sounds Margaret could hear were the crickets outside and the faint rumble of a car's engine somewhere in the distance.

"Meggy..."

The intensity of his voice scared her. "What is it?"

"These past few days with you... they've been the best days of my life."

Joy, spiked and sweet, arrowed through her. "I . . . they've been the best days of my life, too." Her voice shook a little.

"You know what else I was thinking?"

"What?"

"How much I'd like to take you to New York this weekend."

"Oh, Caleb!" Margaret said, delighted.

"Do you have any jobs scheduled?"

"No, I don't!" Could she go? Could she possibly go? She would have to lie to her mother again.

"Why are you frowning?" Caleb said. "Don't you want to go?"

"Oh, God, I'd *love* to go." Just the thought of going into the city with Caleb thrilled her. They could walk in Central Park. Maybe even do the corny tourist things Anthony never had wanted to do, like ride in a hansom cab, eat at Tavern on the Green, ride the Staten Island Ferry. Margaret could just see herself and Caleb strolling along Columbus Circle, looking at the paintings of the street artists, having bagels and coffee at a sidewalk café.

"Then what's the problem?"

Margaret sighed. "I was just thinking about what I could tell my family."

"How about you're going to New York with a friend."

Margaret nodded, but she knew her mother. Her mother would want to know which friend.

"Okay, that's settled," he said. "Tomorrow, right after my last class, I'll come by and pick you up. We'll plan to leave around five."

Then his arms tightened around her, and he was kissing her again, and Margaret stopped thinking.

When Margaret opened her eyes, the bedroom was bright.

Too bright.

She extricated herself from Caleb's arms and sat up. She looked at the clock on the wall.

"Omigod," she said. It was eight forty-five. "Caleb!" She shook his shoulder. "Caleb, wake up!"

"Wha?" he said, sleepily turning over.

"Caleb," she said urgently. "Wake up! It's almost nine o'clock!" Although last night Margaret had told herself she didn't care who saw them, or what anyone thought, she felt suddenly panicky at the idea that her neighbors would probably be out and about and someone was sure to see Caleb leave. She guessed she wasn't quite as brave as she'd thought she was.

Caleb rubbed his eyes and sat up slowly. The sheet covering him slipped down, and even though Margaret's stomach had tightened with nerves, a part of her still admired the smooth, muscled contours of his body. If things were different, she thought, he could stay until it was time for his first class.

"When is your first class?" she asked.

He tossed the sheet aside and stood.

Margaret unabashedly looked at his naked body. Anthony had never stood around naked. He simply wasn't the type. He wasn't ashamed of his body or anything, but it seemed to be second nature to him to automatically reach for his robe when he got up.

Caleb seemed to have no such compunction. He stood there, grinning down at her. His dark hair was tousled and a lock of it fell forward across his face. His blue eyes, clear even this early in the morning, held warmth as he watched her watching him. "My first class isn't until eleven. I've got plenty of time."

What the heck. He was here. What did it matter if he left now or an hour from now? She might as well cook him some breakfast. She smiled at him. "Hungry?"

He patted his flat stomach. "I'm always hungry."

Margaret swung her feet out of bed, and she *did* reach for her robe, which she'd had the foresight to lay within reaching distance the day before. "There are clean towels in the hall closet, if you want to shower. I'll go down and start breakfast. What do you want? Eggs and bacon or pancakes and bacon?"

"Pancakes. Oh . . . and Meggy?"

Margaret turned.

The corners of his mouth twitched. "You sure do look cute in the morning."

Margaret blushed.

Caleb laughed out loud.

Margaret placed the plate of bacon in the microwave, punched in the codes and pressed Start. Then, humming, she walked over to the opposite counter and finished measuring the ingredients for pancakes.

She had just placed the griddle on the stove and turned on the gas when she heard the unmistakable sound of a car's engine coming up the driveway.

Her heart leapt into her throat.

She stood on tiptoe and looked out the window over the sink.

"Oh, dear God," she said as she recognized Lisa's silver car. Her heart knocked against her ribs as she looked wildly around.

The kitchen table was set for two.

Caleb's suit jacket was draped over one of the chairs, his tie neatly laid across it.

Margaret dropped the spatula she'd been holding.

Butter sizzled in the griddle.

The kitchen clocked ticked alarmingly loudly.

A car door slammed. Any minute, there would be a knock at the back door.

Margaret swallowed. Then, moving with lightning speed, she whipped the second serving plate and utensils off the table and shoved them into the nearest cupboard. Grabbing Caleb's suit coat and tie, she looked around wildly, then wadded them into a ball and thrust them into the refrigerator.

The expected knock came.

Margaret took two deep breaths, walked into the utility room and unlocked the back door.

"Hi, Mom!" Lisa smiled. She looked pretty and fresh in a green checked maternity sundress and matching green-framed glasses. "Did you buy a new car?" Lisa nodded in the direction of Caleb's convertible.

"Uh ... no." Margaret thought fast. "It belongs to a friend. Listen, Lisa, come on in and sit down. I'll be right back. I think I left the water running upstairs."

"Okay," Lisa said. She walked over to the stove. "Your butter's burning."

"Turn off the gas, okay?" Margaret had almost made it out the door and into the hall when, just as clear as church bells, Caleb's laughing voice called out, "Meggy! What did you do with my underwear?" and he came bounding down the stairs.

Margaret froze, her back to her daughter. The next few seconds passed in a blur as Caleb, one of Margaret's dark green bath towels knotted around his hips, walked toward her in the hallway. He stopped abruptly when he saw the look on her face. "What's the matter?" he said. "Did something happen?"

"Mother?" Lisa said, walking up behind Margaret.

Margaret met Caleb's startled gaze and then, feeling as if all of this were happening to someone else, she slowly turned.

Lisa's face mirrored her emotions perfectly. First confusion. Then a dawning awareness as she took in Caleb and his attire. Then shock and something else. Something that caused a hard knot of pain in Margaret's breast.

Lisa's throat worked. The color drained from her face. "I—I can't believe this," she whispered. "You . . . you . . . who *is* this man?"

"Uh . . . listen, Margaret, I think I'll just go upstairs . . ." Caleb said.

Margaret heard him retreat. She knew she should say something, but she couldn't think of anything to say. At that moment, she wished she could just crawl into the woodwork and stay there forever.

"Lisa," she began, "let's go sit down, okay?" She reached out to touch her daughter's shoulder.

Lisa stiffened, and her green eyes, so like her grandmother's, glittered. "You're *sleeping* with him, aren't you?" she said, her voice hard and filled with disgust. "I can't *believe* it!" She plopped herself on one of the kitchen chairs and stared at Margaret.

Margaret gathered her robe around her carefully as she seated herself across from Lisa. She struggled for the right words. "Lisa, I know it looks—"

"I'll tell you *exactly* how it looks!" Lisa said. "It looks as if my very own mother has lost her mind! Have you forgotten that Daddy has only been dead a few months?"

"I think that's an exaggeration, don't you?" Margaret said with as much dignity as she could muster.

"Your father has been dead over eight months. That's three-quarters of a year."

"How could you *do* it, Mother?" Lisa wailed. Margaret could see that she was on the verge of tears. "I mean, *Daddy!*"

Love and compassion mixed in with the deep regret Margaret felt. Lisa had adored her father. Anthony, in turn, had doted on her from the moment she was born. He and Tony had been at sword's point most of the time, and Lori had been too much of a rebel, but Lisa had been Anthony's little darling, and she had thought he was perfect. Margaret could see how what Lisa had discovered today might seem like a betrayal of her father. "Darling," Margaret said, "I know it's probably hard for you to understand. Most children don't think of their parents as real people with needs and lives other than in relation to them, but—"

"Oh, don't start spouting that psychobabble at me, Mother!" Lisa exclaimed, jumping up. "I'm not stupid. I can see what happened. Don't try to pretty it up. You got the hots for some young guy, and you forgot all about the husband who loved you and you started screwing some *stranger*—"

Margaret stood so fast she knocked her chair over. "Don't you talk to me like that, young lady," she said through clenched teeth. Her heart pounded furiously, and she fought her own tears. "Don't you *ever* talk to me like that. You have absolutely no right, *no right,* to say things like that. Your father is dead. Dead. Do you understand? And I'm alive. I have a perfect right to see someone else."

Lisa's eyes filled with tears, and her chin quivered.

"Lisa," Margaret said wearily, all the fight gone out of her, "please, honey, can't we talk about this like two adults? Do we have to shout at each other?"

"I don't have anything else to say to you, Mother," Lisa said tightly. She swiped at a tear that crept down her cheek. "I'm leaving now. Goodbye." She swung around and marched out, slamming the back door behind her.

Margaret, trembling and shaken to the core, just stood there. The world moved on around her. The refrigerator hummed. The clock ticked. The house creaked. Outside the window, she could see a tiny wren perch on the windowsill. She heard Lisa's engine rev, heard the squeal of her tires as she backed out of the driveway too fast.

Please, God, let her drive safely, she prayed.

The tears she'd been suppressing rolled down her cheeks, and she felt hot all over.

"Meggy, darling..."

Caleb had walked up behind her, and she felt his strong arms enfolding her. She turned and buried her face in his chest. The tears came in a rush. "Oh, Caleb," she said brokenly.

"I know. I know. I heard most of it." He stroked her hair. "Shh. Don't cry. It'll be all right."

"It...it was so awful."

"I know. But give her some time. She was just shocked, that's all. She'll get over it."

"It was worse than I'd imagined."

He lifted her head and smiled tenderly. "Here," he said, reaching behind him for a tissue. "Blow your nose and dry your eyes. Let's have some coffee and some of that breakfast you promised me. Things will look better once you've had something to eat."

The thought of food nauseated Margaret. All she could see was the stricken look on Lisa's face, the disgust in her eyes, the uncompromising stiffness of her shoulders as she'd stalked away.

"Caleb, I can't. I'm sorry, but would you please just get dressed and go home?"

"Ah, Meggy..." He tried to put his arms around her again, but she pushed him away.

"Please, Caleb. I have to be alone." Suddenly Margaret remembered her lunch date with her mother. "Oh, God," she moaned. Would Lisa call her grandmother? Oh, surely not.

He sighed. "Okay. I'll go. But not for long." He tipped her chin up and gazed into her eyes. "Remember, we're leaving for New York at five."

Margaret swallowed. She had forgotten about New York. "I—I'm not sure—"

"We're going, Margaret. It'll do you good to get away. Especially after what just happened." He kissed her hard. Then he chuckled and said, "Now where have you hidden my coat?"

Chapter Ten

"Margaret, you seem very preoccupied. Is something wrong?"

Margaret shook herself. "No, Mother. I was just thinking, that's all." *No, Mother, there's not a thing wrong. My daughter just hates me, that's all. My entire life is probably going to come crashing down, especially when you find out what's going on, that's all. But there's nothing wrong!*

Joyce's eyes narrowed and she took a sedate bite of her broiled red snapper.

Margaret took a forkful of her Caesar salad. It tasted like weeds. She laid down her fork and glanced out the window. The lush green of the golf course sparkled under the noonday sun. Several golf carts were visible, and on the nearest green, she saw a foursome approaching. Clinking silverware, the hum of conversation and sudden bursts of laughter surrounded them. Just an ordinary day at the Riverview Country Club.

Margaret sighed and turned toward her mother again. Joyce's green eyes met hers squarely. "Are you *sure* you're all right?" she said.

Margaret nodded. "I think I'm just tired. As... as a matter of fact, I've decided to go down to the city for the weekend. I think I need a change of scenery."

"By yourself?"

Margaret lifted her water glass and took a swallow before answering. "Don't worry about me, Mother. I'm forty-five years old. I can handle New York City on my own if I have to."

"Well," her mother said reflectively, "perhaps you're right. You probably *do* need a change of pace. I know how I felt after your father died. It was very difficult for a while."

Margaret nodded noncommittally.

"Besides that, I think you've been working too hard." Joyce smiled. "Are you planning to see any shows or just shop?"

"I don't know. I think I'll just play it by ear."

"Will you be coming back Sunday night?"

"Yes."

"Be sure to call me when you get home."

"It might be late."

"Not *too* late, I hope. I don't like the idea of you driving alone late at night."

"Mother..."

"All right, all right, but I *do* worry about you, Margaret. You've never done much on your own before. You always had dear Anthony to look out for you."

Margaret astounded herself by saying, "Why do you always say 'dear Anthony'? I happen to know you didn't even like him."

Joyce stared at her. Under her immaculate makeup, her cheeks looked pinker, and Margaret knew she was angry. "What is wrong with you, Margaret?" she said in a carefully controlled voice. "Why would you ever say a thing like that?"

Margaret wadded her napkin. She felt ridiculously close to tears again. She could feel her heart beating too fast. She met her mother's gaze and said softly, "I guess I was just hoping that for once in our lives we could be honest with each other."

"Honest with each other? Margaret Jane Guthrie Desmond, I am ashamed of you! Why, I have *always* been honest with you." Her face twisted. "Are you getting ready to have your period, or something?"

Margaret looked down at her plate. She stared unseeingly at her neglected salad. Finally she nodded. "Yes, that's probably it. I'm getting ready to have my period. Or something."

Caleb couldn't get the image of Margaret's anguished eyes out of his mind.

It was funny, he thought as he closed up his office for the weekend and hurried home to get ready for their trip. What had happened this morning was serious, no doubt about it, at least in Margaret's eyes. But the confrontation between Margaret and her daughter had shown Caleb something.

He had discovered Margaret was even more important to him than he'd thought.

He had discovered, when he'd looked into her beautiful eyes swimming with tears, that he didn't want to lose her.

He had discovered, as he'd held her trembling body and soothed her, that what he felt for her was more than physical desire.

He had discovered that he was falling in love with her.

Margaret decided, as she threw some clothes into a small suitcase, that as long as the fat was already in the fire, she might as well get as much out of these few days alone with Caleb as she could.

I am going to have a wonderful time, she vowed.

Caleb showed up at five minutes after five. His eyes held a peculiar expression, not just concern for how she might be feeling, but something else.

Margaret gave him her jauntiest smile. "I'm okay," she said. "I know you were probably worried about me."

"I was." He touched her cheek, then bent down to kiss it lightly. "Are you ready?"

"Umm-hmm." She pointed to her little suitcase.

"Is that all you're taking?"

"I figured if I needed anything else, I'd buy it."

He grinned. "That's my girl."

It was less than two hundred miles from Riverview into downtown Manhattan, and they made good time. By eight-thirty, they were crossing the George Washington Bridge, and the lights of Manhattan were strewn before them like jewels. By nine o'clock, they'd exited the Henry Hudson Parkway and had relinquished the keys of Caleb's car to the valet parking attendant at the Marriott Marquis Hotel on Broadway.

"I've never stayed here before," Margaret said as their glass-enclosed elevator deposited them at the eighth floor lobby. "It's beautiful."

Caleb smiled. "It is, isn't it?"

Margaret's eyes widened when she saw that they had a suite on the thirty-seventh floor. "Caleb," she said. "My God, this must be costing you a small fortune!"

He grinned. "I have connections."

Margaret walked to the window and looked out. The city stretched forever. To her left she could just see the lights of Times Square.

Caleb walked up behind her, put his arms around her, and Margaret sank back against him. It felt good to be held this way. "What kind of connections?" she said lazily. "Did you date the owner's daughter, or something?"

He chuckled and dipped his head to kiss her neck. "No, better than that."

Margaret turned in his arms, looked up into his laughing eyes.

"My brother works here. In the sales department. He gave me a good rate."

"See? It pays to have a big family sometimes, doesn't it?" Margaret said, laughing herself. Then she said, "Oh, no. Now *your* family will know about us, too!"

"Yeah, but *they* won't care. In fact," Caleb said ruefully, "they'll probably think it's about time I found a woman like you."

Margaret smiled and pushed the thoughts of her mother's disapproving face and her daughter's shocked one out of her mind. Time enough for that on Sunday. "Will I get to meet your brother?" she asked.

"Not unless we make a trip out to Long Island where he lives. He doesn't work on the weekends."

"Oh, too bad. I would've enjoyed meeting him." Margaret wondered if Caleb's brothers and sisters were anything like him.

"If you really want to, I suppose I could arrange it, but I kind of wanted you to myself on this trip." He smiled down into her eyes. "I'm not ready to share you with anyone."

Margaret smiled.

"So what do you want to do first?" Caleb added, still holding her lightly. "Make love or . . . make love?"

"Why don't we make love?"

They did all the things Margaret had imagined they'd do. After making love on Friday night, they'd showered together, dressed in jeans and athletic shoes and headed down to the street level of the big hotel.

They walked hand in hand along 46th Street until they came to a small Chinese restaurant. They ate, then walked out into the warm night air and mingled with the after-theater crowd. About midnight, they slowly headed back to the hotel.

The following morning, they got up early. "We don't want to waste the day, do we?" Margaret chided as Caleb tried to bury his head under his pillow in protest.

They ate a leisurely breakfast in the hotel, then walked out onto the sunny streets. All morning they walked, stopping here and there, as the spirit moved them.

Toward noon, Margaret spied a street vendor. "Oh, Caleb, I want a hot dog."

He bought her one loaded with sauerkraut and mustard. It tasted wonderful.

When she'd finished eating and thrown her napkin into a nearby trash bin, Caleb chuckled. "You have mustard on your chin."

Margaret raised her hand to wipe it off.

"I'll do it," he said. Then, ignoring the people jostling them on the sidewalk, he bent down and licked her chin. Margaret got the funniest feeling in the pit of her stomach. He straightened, and they looked into each other's eyes. Wordlessly they headed back to the hotel.

Later they got dressed up, and Caleb took her to see "Crazy For You." When the heroine sang "Someone to Watch Over Me," Margaret got a lump in her throat and reached for Caleb's hand.

They ate a late supper at Tavern on the Green, just as Margaret had wished, then, humoring her again, Caleb hired a hansom cab and they rode through Central Park.

Saturday night, when Caleb made love to her, bringing her to one of those exquisitely shattering peaks of pleasure, Margaret held him tightly and tears slid down her cheeks.

"Meggy...darling Meggy, why are you crying?" he whispered. He brushed the tears away.

"I wish we could stay here forever," she said, an aching sadness almost overwhelming her.

He held her close and stroked her hair. "Hide out, you mean."

She nodded, knowing she was a coward but not able to help herself. He continued to stroke her hair. She wondered if he was disgusted with her. He was probably used to brave women who defied the world. Margaret wished she could be that way. Wished she could tell her children and her mother and anyone else who had anything to say about the way she lived her life to go to the devil.

"Do you realize," he said, "that it's only been one week since we picnicked at the river?"

It felt like a whole lifetime to Margaret.

On Sunday, Margaret's sadness was gone. She woke up determined to enjoy the day. Whatever happened when she got home, happened. She would deal with it somehow.

After a leisurely lunch at Rockefeller Center, where Caleb insisted Margaret try the crab cakes, they strolled Fifth Avenue and ended the afternoon at a sidewalk café where they ate lemon ice.

Finally, about five, Caleb said, "We'd better start back, don't you think?"

It was nearly midnight before they pulled into Margaret's driveway. Caleb automatically drove toward the back, but Margaret said, "Caleb, stop."

He did, then turned to look at her.

"Please don't take this the wrong way," she said, "but I don't want you to stay over tonight."

He nodded, his eyes a dark gleam in the moonlight.

He walked her to the front door, and Margaret, feeling weird and oddly defiant, let him kiss her on the front stoop, under the outside light, in full view of anyone who cared to look.

"Call me after your classes tomorrow?" she said as he turned to go.

"You can count on it."

Once Caleb's car lights disappeared, Margaret locked the front door, set her bag down, then slowly walked to the telephone table in the hall. She looked down and saw that the light was blinking.

She pressed the Message button.

"Hi, Margaret," said Rosemary's voice. "I guess you're not in. Call me when you get home, okay?"

The phone beeped.

"Margaret? This is Betty Flack. I just wanted to talk to you in more detail about Punky's party. Will you please call me when you get home?"

The phone beeped again.

"Margaret?"

Margaret's blood froze. It was her mother's voice.

"I don't care *what* time you arrive home, you call me the *instant* you get in. Do you hear me?"

The phone beeped five times, the tape rewound, then the instrument went still.

Margaret bit her bottom lip and stared at the silent phone. Then very slowly, like a woman in a dream, she bent down, unplugged it and walked back to the kitchen. Three unplugged phones later, she turned off the lights and climbed into bed.

The doorbell rang at eight o'clock the following morning. Margaret sat up in bed. She looked at the bedside clock. Then she got up and walked to the front window. Parting the drapes, she gazed down at the street.

Her mother's black car sat in the middle of the driveway. Knowing there was no escape, Margaret reached for her robe.

"Good morning, Margaret," her mother said when she opened the front door. Her mouth settled into a tight, unforgiving line, and her green eyes looked like two chips of ice. She stepped inside, brushing huffily past Margaret.

"Why don't you come in, Mother?" Margaret said.

"If I were you, I wouldn't be quite so flippant." As early as it was, Joyce looked impeccable in a crisp blue skirt and blue-and-white striped blouse.

Margaret told herself to be calm. *Don't say anything you'll regret.*

Joyce marched straight back to the kitchen. "I could do with a cup of coffee," she said.

"Fine," Margaret said. "I'll put a pot on, then. If you don't mind, I plan to go upstairs, wash my face, brush my teeth and comb my hair."

Joyce sat down, her face stony.

The temptation to dawdle was strong, but Margaret resisted. Five minutes later, she was back downstairs. The coffee was nearly ready, and Margaret saw that her mother had already gotten out the mugs and cream and sugar.

When they were both settled at the table with their coffee, Margaret said, "Okay, Mother. Say your piece."

"Have you lost your mind, Margaret?"

Margaret took a sip of her coffee and forced herself to meet her mother's gaze without flinching. "I don't think so," she replied quietly.

"Well, I do. What other possible explanation could there be for you to completely disregard the rules of civilized society and positively *flaunt* this unsuitable liaison with that *professor* in the faces of your mother, your children and your friends?"

"Oh, for heaven's sake—"

"Don't 'for heaven's sake' me, Margaret! Don't try to make light of this. Don't try to make me look like *I'm* the one in the wrong, here." Joyce's eyes no longer looked icy. Now they flashed with heat as she got more wound up.

Margaret's head felt as if her mother were hammering it with steel instead of words.

"Do you have any *idea* how upset your pregnant daughter is?" Joyce said. "Do you have any conception at all of how much you've hurt her? What is *wrong* with you, Margaret? Sneaking around. Lying to me. Having *sex* with a man barely older than your son! And in your husband's *bed!*"

Margaret stared at her mother.

"Why, you even went to New York with him this weekend, didn't you? I asked you if you were going alone, and you out and out *lied* to me."

"I didn't lie to you, Mother. I just neglected to answer your question directly. And Caleb is not *barely* older than Tony, and you know it. Tony is only twenty-four, and Caleb is thirty-seven."

"Don't play word games with me. You know what I mean."

"Yes, you're right. I do know what you mean. And yes, you're right again. I did go to New York with Caleb." Margaret lifted her chin, anger forcing out the dread and anxiety she'd felt upon first seeing her mother. "And you know what? I had a wonderful time. The best time I've ever had, anywhere, with anyone. And if he asked me to go again, I would."

Joyce stood up, knocking over her mug and spilling her coffee. Both women ignored the spreading liquid, even when it dripped onto the tile floor. "I think you're having a breakdown," Joyce said. Her chest heaved as she fought to control herself.

Margaret stood, too. "Are you finished, Mother? Have you said everything you came to say?"

"Margaret, I don't understand you. What has this man *done* to you?" Joyce peered at her closely. "Are you on drugs? Has he gotten you hooked on—"

"What are you *talking* about!" Margaret couldn't believe it. She simply couldn't believe it. "Just *listen* to yourself, Mother. No, I'm not taking drugs. Caleb would never do anything to hurt me. I can't believe you said that!"

Her mother's face flushed, and Margaret knew she was embarrassed. Good. She should be. What she'd insinuated was unforgivable.

"You know," Margaret said, struggling to calm down, "I think it might be best if you leave now. Before either of us says anything worse."

"I have no intention of leaving until I've talked some sense into you!"

"You're not talking," Margaret said quietly. "You're shouting. Now, whether you go or not is entirely up to you. I, however, intend to go upstairs and take a shower, then I plan to get dressed and go out." Margaret wasn't sure where she was going, but anything was better than staying home and being subjected to this.

Leaving her mother sputtering, Margaret left the kitchen—not even staying long enough to wipe up the spilled coffee—and went upstairs. She firmly closed the door to her bedroom, and for the first time in her life, locked the door. She made it inside the bathroom before she broke down.

An hour later, dry-eyed, hair fixed, makeup on and dressed in a khaki jumpsuit with a narrow red belt and red leather flats, Margaret slowly walked downstairs.

Her mother was gone, and the coffee was wiped up. Joyce had even shut off the coffeemaker.

A note sat in the middle of the kitchen table, anchored by the sugar bowl.

Margaret,

Although you said some awful things to me, I forgive you. I know you're not yourself. I'm going to ask your sister to talk to you. Maybe she can get you to come to your senses.

Mother

Margaret wadded up the note and tossed it into the wastebasket.

She left the phones unplugged.

"Margaret! Hi! I called you Saturday. Did you get my message?"

"Yes, I did." Margaret smiled at Rosemary with the first sense of real pleasure she'd had so far that day. As usual, Rosemary looked terrific. Today she wore a bold black-and-white geometric print dress that ended a couple of inches above her knees, and Margaret saw a white picture hat with black band adorning the top of the clothes tree in the corner of her office.

"Sit down." Rosemary gestured to the gray suede chairs grouped to the side of her desk. "Would you like some coffee? I'll ask Sandra to get some for you."

Margaret shook her head. "No, I just..." She glanced at the open door. "Could we shut the door?"

Rosemary's eyes widened. "Sure." She stood, indicating with her hand that Margaret should stay seated. After shutting the door, she walked over and sat in the chair next to Margaret. She crossed her legs and leaned forward. "What's going on?" Her dark eyes were filled with concern and friendship.

Margaret's tenuous hold on self-control nearly snapped in the face of Rosemary's warmth. She took a deep breath and willed herself not to cry. "Friday morning, I had a terrible confrontation with Lisa. And about an hour ago, I had an even uglier one with my mother. Both of them think I've lost my mind. My mother accused me of being on drugs." Margaret met Rosemary's incredulous gaze. "She asked me if Caleb had gotten me 'hooked' on something."

"Oh, my," Rosemary said. She whistled.

"And Lisa accused me of forgetting all about the husband who loved me and screwing some stranger."

This time Rosemary's mouth popped open.

Margaret grimaced. "Think how I felt."

"Whoa," Rosemary said. "They sure don't pull any punches, do they?"

Margaret tried to smile, but her bottom lip quivered, and she had to bite it to keep from bursting into tears all over again.

Rosemary reached over and took Margaret's hands in hers. She squeezed gently. "Listen, Magpie," she said softly and urgently, "what you do is your business. Nobody else's. Whether you're sleeping with Caleb or anyone else is not your mother's or your daughter's affair. Hell, didn't you tell me that Lisa had gotten herself involved with some jerk before she married Keith? I seem to remember she was real hot to trot, and she didn't listen to you when you tried to talk to her. If I recall, she said she was old enough to make her own choices."

Margaret had forgotten about that episode. But Lisa had said exactly that.

"Well, my dear," Rosemary said, "you are *definitely* old enough to make your own choices. Tell your daughter to put that in her pipe and smoke it!"

Margaret smiled.

"There! That's better! Laughing is better than crying any day."

"What do you advise me to tell my mother?" Margaret asked.

"I think what you should tell your mother is probably unprintable," Rosemary muttered. Then she grinned. "Tell her you think she's in dire need of an enema."

Margaret hooted. She could just imagine what her mother's face would look like if Margaret were to say any such thing.

Rosemary leaned forward and hugged her. When she sat back again, she looked at Margaret speculatively. "Do you want to tell me what brought on all this emotional turmoil?"

Margaret sighed. "Well, would you believe that Lisa showed up at the house Friday morning and discovered Caleb there—dressed in nothing but a towel?"

"Omistars," Rosemary said, clapping her hand over her mouth. Her dark eyes sparkled with merriment. "*That* must have been an eyeful."

Even though it wasn't really funny, Margaret laughed. "Yes," she said, "Caleb in a towel is a sight to behold." Sobering, she added, "And my mother, well, Lisa must have called her because Mother said 'I'd upset my pregnant daughter terribly' but she was also furious because I'd lied to her." Margaret met Rosemary's gaze again. "See, I went to New York with Caleb for the weekend. I told Mother I was going, but

I neglected to say Caleb would be with me. When she asked me if I was going alone, I evaded the question."

"Uh-*huh*. Well, I can see how Old Ironsides would get a little miffed over that."

"Old Ironsides?" Margaret asked. "Is that what you call my mother?"

Rosemary grinned. "That's what *everyone* calls your mother, Margaret. Surely you knew that."

Margaret started to laugh again, but then the laugh turned to a moan. "Oh, God, Ro, what am I going to *do?*"

"Hey, kiddo, if I were you, I wouldn't do a darned thing. Seems to me it's your daughter and your mother who have the problem, not you." Rosemary cocked her head. "What does Caleb say about all this?"

"He doesn't know about my mother. He overheard most of what Lisa had to say, of course. He thinks pretty much along the same lines you do. It's nobody's business but ours."

"And he's right."

"Sometimes being right is no comfort." Margaret gave Rosemary a grateful smile. "But I appreciate your advice, anyway. Now, I guess, I've got a lot of thinking to do."

Chapter Eleven

Caleb felt antsy all day. It wasn't until he reached the privacy of the carriage house and could call Margaret that he settled down.

The phone rang and rang and rang and no one answered.

That was strange, he thought. He knew Margaret had an answering machine. And she'd said to call her after his classes were over.

He decided to change his clothes and drive over to her house. Maybe by the time he did, she'd be home. Just as he started to walk back to his bedroom, the phone rang.

"Caleb?"

"Margaret! I just tried to call you."

"I'm not at home."

Now he could hear the muffled noises in the background. "Where are you?"

"It doesn't matter. Listen, Caleb, can you meet me? I need to talk to you."

"Sure. Where?"

"How about at the river? The same spot where we had our picnic."

"When?"

"Fifteen minutes?"

Caleb frowned as he hung up the phone. Something was wrong. Margaret hadn't sounded like herself. He tried to banish the sudden feeling of foreboding that stole through him.

He didn't bother changing his clothes. He just locked up, jumped on his bike and took off toward the river.

When he arrived, she was already there, sitting on a flat boulder at the edge of the water. His heart contracted at the sight of her. She looked so forlorn and so heart-wrenchingly beautiful. She was in profile to him, the classic lines of her face and throat brushed by the sun glinting off the river. Pine needles crunched underfoot, and she looked up and met his gaze. Her eyes were filled with something indescribably sad. Caleb's feeling of foreboding ballooned into full-fledged fear.

"Meggy, what's wrong?" he said as he reached her side.

She stood. They looked at each other for a long moment, then Margaret said, "Oh, Caleb, I don't know what to do. All day I've been thinking and thinking, and I just don't know what to do."

Caleb gathered her close, and he could feel how her body trembled. "What's happened?"

"My mother is furious with me, and my daughter feels as if I've betrayed her, and I'm sure when they get through talking to the rest of my family, they'll all be upset and angry with me, too."

"Because of me?"

"Yes. They think I'm making a fool of myself. They think it's disgraceful that I'm seeing someone so soon after Anthony died. Especially someone so...young." She hung her head. "I don't know, Caleb. All day I've been thinking and thinking. Maybe...maybe we *should* stop seeing each other."

Caleb's heart knocked against his ribs. Everything in him cried out in protest. He tipped her face up and searched her eyes. "No," he said. "No." He kissed her then, and Margaret clung to him. There was a desperate quality to the kiss, because Caleb was afraid.

The sound of approaching footsteps was the only reason he broke the kiss. Over Margaret's shoulder, he saw several young people coming toward them, walking along the footpath that bordered the river. He put his arm protectively around Margaret's shoulders and turned her so that their backs were to the approaching teenagers.

When the kids had passed and they were alone again, Caleb said, "Meggy, there's something I want to tell you."

She looked up. Caleb cupped her face in his hands. "I won't let you go without a fight," he said. "I can't. I never thought this would happen to me, but... I've fallen in love with you."

Her throat worked. "Caleb, you hardly know me."

"I know everything I need to know."

"No. No, you don't. I come with a lot of extra baggage."

"It doesn't matter." His feelings were beginning to be a little hurt by her reaction to his declaration. "Meggy, don't you *want* me to be in love with you?"

"Oh, God, Caleb," she said with an anguished cry. "Don't you see that this just makes things harder for me right now? I'm so confused. I don't know how I feel about you. Whether I'm just bemused by the attention or bedazzled by the—" her face colored "—the terrific sex or bedeviled by some kind of urge to defy convention!"

"I thought that line went bewitched, bothered and bewildered," he said.

"That, too," she said.

"You're not scaring me off, you know."

"Caleb . . ."

"I think you're in love with me, too, but you're afraid to admit it."

She pushed herself away, and he let her go, reluctant to hold her against her will. "Don't put pressure on me, too," she said, so low he almost didn't hear it.

Caleb sighed. "All right, Meggy. You win. No pressure. But I've told you how I feel, and I mean it. Now, I guess, it's up to you."

It's up to you.

All the way home Caleb's parting remark played in her mind—a challenge, a taunt, a reminder that she had the power to make her own choices.

He had declared himself. Thrown down the gauntlet. It was up to her whether or not she picked it up.

Margaret sighed, wishing she didn't have to go home. Wishing she could just hole up somewhere, by herself, for about a week. If she could be perfectly still and all alone, maybe she could sort everything out. Figure out what was right and what was wrong. Who was right, and who was wrong.

But she had to go home. She knew she couldn't avoid her house forever.

What was she going to do?

She was more confused than ever. Caleb's declaration of love should have made things easier for her. Instead, as she'd told him, it only made things harder.

Now she had to make a decision.

In the back of her mind, she had never expected their relationship to be anything more than a brief and memorable experience. She had never thought it would impact her life in any meaningful and ongoing way. She had never thought she would be the one to decide on its outcome.

That was the *real* trouble, she admitted ruefully. She hadn't really thought at all. She had simply acted.

Now she would pay the consequences.

Part of her knew, if she wanted her life to stay on any kind of even keel, she should stop seeing Caleb immediately. The other part of her, the part that had just begun to emerge, cried out against this sensible solution to her dilemma.

Was she in love with Caleb, then? She didn't know if he had expected her to say she was in love with him, too, when he'd made his declaration, or if he had simply wanted her to know the depth of his feelings for her.

That was the other problem. She didn't know Caleb well enough to know *what* he expected. How could she? She'd only known him a little over a week, and she'd spent most of her time with him in bed.

Oh, God. Was her mother right? Was she crazy? Was this behavior simply some kind of midlife crisis—a last fling before entering the full throes of middle age?

A last fling? Margaret, you've never even had a first fling!

Maybe that was the crux of her problems. Maybe if she hadn't led such a boring, circumspect life for the past forty-five years, she wouldn't have been so quick to fall into the bed of the first good-looking man who gave her the eye.

But as soon as the thought formed, Margaret rejected it. It simply wasn't true, and she knew it. Caleb wasn't the first good-looking man to give her the eye since Anthony's death. Several months earlier, a handsome, fiftyish graphic artist who had helped her design her business cards had openly propositioned her, and she hadn't even been tempted. She'd just been embarrassed and couldn't wait to make her escape.

She was still wrestling with her conflicting feelings and the confusion and unhappiness caused by Lisa's and her mother's reaction to her relationship with Caleb when she turned onto her street and approached her house.

"Oh, no," she moaned, spying the vehicle parked in front of her house. "That's *all* I need today. A visit from my loving sister."

Margaret tooted her horn and waved, just as if it was an ordinary day. By the time she'd pulled into the garage and gotten out of the car, Madelyn was walking purposefully up the driveway toward her.

Margaret studied her sister, thinking how any stranger, looking at the two of them together, would never guess they were related. Madelyn's hair was dark, like their father's had been in his youth, and she kept it cut short and wore it in a sleek cap. Her eyes were also dark, almost black, a throwback to some ancestor no one remembered, Margaret guessed. Madelyn was taller than Margaret and bigger-boned, again, built like their father had been. She also possessed his drive and intelligence and was strikingly attractive in a bold, no-nonsense way. But in her personality, she was exactly like their mother. Completely self-assured and confident and certain she was right about everything. From the time she was born, when Margaret was five, Madelyn had been a thorn in her older sister's side.

She and Margaret had never had anything in common. Even though Madelyn was younger, she intimidated Margaret, who was always disgusted with herself for feeling that way. Margaret very obviously bored Madelyn, who barely managed to conceal her impatience and disinterest in Margaret's life, thoughts, or opinions.

Still, Margaret had always tried to maintain the fiction of familial warmth, and she did so now. "Hi," she said, giving Madelyn a bright smile. "What brings you here during office hours?"

"Let's not play games," Madelyn said. Her eyes were chilly as they met Margaret's. "We both know Mother asked me to come. She said maybe you'd listen to me if no one else."

Would it kill her sister to smile? Would it kill her to pretend she had some real feeling for Margaret? What gave her the right to be so judgmental, anyway? A long-buried resentment flooded Margaret. "And so, of course, you jumped at the chance to lecture me."

Madelyn gave her a long-suffering look, and when she spoke her tone was that of wise parent to rebellious child. "Now, Margaret, when you act with thoughtless disregard for everyone who cares about you, you have to expect to be lectured. We're only concerned with your welfare and the welfare of your children, you know."

Margaret gave a weary sigh. "Oh, of course. What else?"

"If this distasteful episode only concerned you, it would be one thing," Madelyn said. "But—"

"Let's go in the house." Margaret interrupted her. "If I'm going to be lectured, I'd rather do it sitting down and out of the neighbors' eyesight."

She didn't look to see if her sister was following her. She knew she'd probably shocked Madelyn with her responses to Madelyn's comments, because in the past, she had never shown much spunk, finding it infinitely easier to agree with her sister and preserve the illusion of harmony.

You've been a total wimp, you know that? I can't imagine why Caleb thinks he loves you.

Remembering the fervency of his avowal gave her a glow of pleasure and a burst of confidence. She unlocked the back door and walked inside, tossing her purse on the kitchen table and heading for the refrigerator. "Do you want a diet drink?" she said as her sister entered the kitchen a few seconds later.

"No, thank you." Madelyn removed her shoulder bag and laid it carefully on the kitchen counter. Instead of sitting at the table, she leaned back against the counter and folded her arms in front of her. In her plain white blouse and dark tailored slacks unsoftened by jewelry or a colorful accent, she looked businesslike and serious. She had once said in Margaret's hearing that any female doctor who wanted to be taken seriously couldn't afford to indulge herself by wearing frivolous or feminine clothing.

Margaret extracted a diet soda from the refrigerator, and in silent defiance of her sister's stance, pulled out a kitchen chair and sat down.

Neither said anything for a long moment. Margaret decided she'd be damned if she'd break the silence. This was her sister's show. Margaret had nothing to say.

Madelyn finally shook her head and sighed audibly. "I can see you're not going to be reasonable."

"If by reasonable you mean do what you want me to do, you're probably right. I think, for once in my life, I'm going to do what I want to do."

Something sparked in Madelyn's eyes, and for a second Margaret thought it might be admiration, then quickly dismissed the thought. That was just wishful thinking.

"Even if that hurts your children?" Madelyn said.

"Maybe if everyone else would mind their own business, Lisa and I would be able to work this out." Now it was Margaret's turn to sigh and her voice softened in a genuine attempt to make Madelyn understand. "Lisa's just hurt. She adored her father, and she thinks I'm betraying his memory." Margaret's gaze met Madelyn's levelly. "You and I both know that Anthony wasn't exactly a perfect husband. He had at least one affair that I know of, and maybe there were others. Anyway, as I told my daughter, I was always faithful and loyal to him while he was alive. Now that he's dead, I don't think I owe him anything. I think Lisa is old enough to understand this, and I wish you and Mother would back off long enough for us to talk without interference from you two."

"I'm not disputing any of that. Actually it's all irrelevant. The thing that concerns Mother, and me, is that you've taken up with someone so completely unsuitable. I did some checking on Caleb Mahoney today after Mother called me, and what I found out didn't make either of us feel better."

"You did some *checking* on him! How dare you?" Margaret said, outrage and a hot sense of shame rushing through her.

"Margaret, when you behave the way you've been behaving, you have to expect your family to take extreme measures. After all, you're a moderately wealthy woman and we feel—"

"Are you insinuating that Caleb is only interested in me because I have some money?" Margaret wanted to throw something at her sister. To blast that smug, superior expression right off her face.

"Oh, come on, Margaret, surely you're not *that* naive. A man like Caleb Mahoney can have his pick of any number of nubile young things. Why should he want a forty-five-year-old woman who's soon going to be a grandmother?"

Margaret stared at her sister. Pain, sharp and intense, pressed against her chest. "Why, indeed?" she whispered. Then, feeling infinitely older than her forty-five years, she stood. "On that cheerful thought, I must bid you goodbye. I have a headache and I'm going upstairs to lie down. You know the way out."

And for the second time that day, she turned her back on a family member and left her standing in the kitchen.

Caleb wished he had someone to talk to. He thought about Jake, but he wasn't ready to tell Jake about Margaret. That only left Kathleen. He decided to call her.

"Gee, I don't know what to tell you," she said after he'd given her a complete rundown on the events of the past week. "Sounds as if you've done everything you can do. Now it's kind of up to Margaret, isn't it?"

"I guess so," Caleb said. He didn't like the feeling of not being in control. It wasn't something he was used to, especially when it came to his relationships with women. In the past, he'd always called the shots.

"I can understand how she must feel," Kathleen added.

"Yeah," he agreed, but privately, he really didn't understand. Why did Margaret *care* so much what other people thought?

"Caleb?"

"What?"

"Are you sure you're not . . ."

"Not what?"

"Just adding another notch to your belt," she said in a rush.

His first inclination was to reply indignantly, but then he sighed and said, "No. I never once thought that. Even that first night, when I tried to get her to go out with me, it was because there was something special about her. Something that appealed to me."

"You sound as if you're in love with her," Kathleen said softly.

"I think I am."

"Caleb, what if your Margaret decides she wants to continue to be with you? What then?"

He frowned. "What do you mean?"

"Well, surely you see that if you really do love her, you need to try to find a way to continue to see her without alienating her entire family. I mean, it's not just you and Margaret that have to be considered. She's got grown children with feelings. She loves them. She doesn't want them to hate her. How happy could she be if that were the case? And Caleb . . ." She hesitated again. "Have you really thought all this out? Are you sure you're ready to take on this kind of problem? Remember, her kids will be her kids forever. And if they don't like you, they can make your life hell.''

Caleb's frown deepened. What Kathleen said made sense. His first feelings of uneasiness crept down his spine. ''Are you saying you think I should back off?''

''No. That has to be your decision. All I'm saying is, give this some serious thought.'' She paused, and he could hear her soft breathing. ''And whatever you decide, good luck.''

''Thanks,'' Caleb said slowly. ''I think I'm going to need it.''

Margaret finally plugged the phone back in about seven o'clock that evening. It rang immediately. She let the answering machine pick up and listened.

''Mother? It's Lori. Are you there?''

She snatched up the phone. ''Lori! Hi, honey. I was wondering when I'd hear from you.''

''I called you a couple of times over the weekend, but you never answered.''

''Why didn't you leave a message?''

''It would be hard for you to call me back. It's not like I have a phone in my *room* or anything, not in this antiquated college.''

This lack of a private phone had been one of Lori's biggest complaints and the reason most vehemently stated in her arguments for an off-campus apartment.

''Well, I'm glad you caught me now,'' Margaret said. She was determined not to be goaded into any kind of disagreement with her youngest daughter. Bad enough that she was barely on speaking terms with her mother, her sister and Lisa. ''How have things been going now that you've had a chance to get settled in?''

"Fine."

"Do you like your classes?"

"They're okay. It's not like this school has such a great drama department or anything."

Margaret told herself to be patient. "I'll bet you've made a lot of new friends."

"Yeah, some. Actually a couple of the guys who live in this dorm are really neat."

"Well, that sounds promising."

"Yeah. Uh, Mother, I heard something a little while ago that seemed really weird."

"Oh? What was that?"

"Well, Judy and a couple of the other kids were down at the river this afternoon, and she said she saw you there."

Margaret clenched the receiver.

"She said—and this is the weird part—that you were, uh, kissing some guy."

Margaret's throat went dry.

"Mother? Are you there?"

Margaret cleared her throat. "Yes, I'm here."

"Isn't that *weird?* I told her it couldn't possibly be you, but she swears it was." Lori laughed, the sound forced and self-conscious. "She said you were really getting it on."

"Uh, maybe we should wait and talk about this when we see each other instead of over the phone."

"You mean . . . it *was* you?" Lori squeaked.

"Yes, Lori, it was me," Margaret said quietly.

"Mother! I can't believe this! Who were you with? Were you really *kissing* him? Making *out?*"

"Judy exaggerated. I kissed him once, and his name isn't important. He—he's a friend of mine."

There was a shocked silence for about two heartbeats, then Lori said, "Holy sh—"

"Don't swear at me, Lori," Margaret said automatically.

"He must be a really *good* friend if you were kissing him. How long has this been going on? Are you having *sex* with him?"

"That's no one's business but mine."

"You *are* having sex with him! God, Mother, what's happening—"

"I *said,* don't swear at me, Lori, and I mean it. If you keep it up, I'll hang up on you."

"Well, pardon *me.*" A strained silence followed.

Margaret waited, carefully keeping her mind blank. She would not get upset. She would not cry. She would not allow her eighteen-year-old daughter to make her feel guilty, too. She heard voices in the background and someone call Lori's name.

"I have to go now, Mother," Lori said, her voice huffy and put-upon.

"All right, Lori."

"Goodbye," Lori said and broke the connection.

Margaret wondered how many more times she would be subjected to someone's shocked silences. The only person left to shock was Tony, and somehow she hoped he would be more tolerant and understanding.

Margaret knew mothers weren't supposed to have favorite children, but she suspected most of them did. Oh, she loved all three of her children equally, but Tony had always been her favorite. Lisa had been an easier child to raise and a model daughter, but Margaret and Tony had always been on the same wavelength. He'd always had the marvelous quality of empathy—that ability to put himself in the other person's shoes.

Margaret would never forget the time he was in the fourth grade, and he'd come home from school with a shiner the size of an orange. Margaret was shocked, because Tony wasn't a fighter. She'd clucked over him and finally gotten him to tell her what happened.

"Some of the kids were picking on Donald," he'd said, indignation firing his eyes, which were the exact shade of Margaret's.

"I see," Margaret said, and she did. Donald was a classmate with a speech impediment. In the cruel way of children, the kids would often mimic him and make fun of him. Tony invariably went to Donald's defense. This time it had obviously gotten physical.

"How would the guys like it if *they* talked like Donald?" Tony asked, outrage causing his voice to rise.

"You're right, honey, they wouldn't like it at all," Margaret said. She'd hugged him and whispered, "Don't ever change, Tony. I love you."

Embarrassed, he'd pulled away.

Yes, Margaret expected Tony to—if not understand—at least try to put himself in her place.

She decided she would not wait for him to call her. She picked up the phone and dialed his number.

"Hi, Mom!" he said.

"Hi."

"I wondered if you'd call," he said.

"I suppose that means you've heard."

He laughed. "Yeah. Lisa called me Friday, Gram called me yesterday and Lori called me today. You sure have gotten everybody stirred up, haven't you?"

Margaret wished he were there so she could hug him the way she had when he was little. "I guess I have. Are you angry with me, too?"

"Aw, come on. You know I'm not like that."

"Your sisters are certainly bent out of shape. You'd think I killed somebody."

"Well, you know...they're just upset 'cause of Dad."

"Tony, your father is dead."

"I know that. Hey, listen, I don't blame you. I don't think there's anything wrong in you going out with a guy."

"Thank you, honey. I appreciate that."

"But Mom..."

Margaret stiffened. Not Tony. Not another lecture.

"You know..." He hesitated. "You're pretty naive. And there are a lot of jerks out there. You've gotta be careful."

"Don't you think I know that? And I'm not as naive as you all seem to think. In fact, I think, now that I'm older, I'm a pretty good judge of character."

"Yeah, well. I don't know. Some guys have a good line. I'm a guy. I know."

Margaret smiled. "Honey, I appreciate your concern, but please believe me. Caleb isn't like that."

They talked for a while longer, then Tony said, "Why don't you come up and spend next weekend with me and Darcy?"

"I have a job booked for next Saturday. A wedding."

"Oh. Well, come during the week. I'm off on Wednesday."

"Thanks for asking, honey. I'll think about it and let you know."

"Okay. Love you, Mom."

"I love you, too."

After they hung up, Margaret thought about their conversation and even though she was a little disappointed Tony hadn't supported her wholeheartedly, at least he hadn't condemned her. At least he'd simply warned her to be careful.

After she went to bed that night, her mind swirled.

Some guys have a good line.

I've fallen in love with you, Meggy.

No! Caleb wasn't like that. Besides, she'd already been to bed with him. What possible motive could he have for telling her he loved her except that it was the truth?

A man like Caleb Mahoney can have his pick of any number of nubile young things. Why should he want a forty-five year old woman who's going to be a grandmother soon?

Margaret squeezed her eyes tight.

You're pretty naive, Mom.

I've fallen in love with you, Meggy.

Margaret finally got up, put on her robe, walked downstairs and through the dark house until she reached the kitchen. She poured herself a glass of milk and stood drinking it as she stared out the back window. Moonlight silvered the lawn and cast mysterious shadows in the corners.

She stood there for a long time, long after the glass was empty, until she finally came to a decision.

The next morning, the first person she called was Caleb.

"Would you like to come for dinner tonight?" she said.

"What time?"

"Seven?"

"Seven it is. And Meggy?"

"Yes?"

"I love you."

The next person she called was Lisa. When Lisa realized who it was her voice cooled.

"I'm sorry I upset you the other day, honey," Margaret said.

"I'm sorry, too."

"I think we need to talk."

"All right."

So far, so good, Margaret thought. "How about if I take you to lunch tomorrow? Someplace really special, like The Inn?"

"All right."

"I'll pick you up at twelve-thirty. How's that?"

Lisa agreed, and they hung up with Margaret feeling hopeful. At least Lisa had agreed to come.

Finally she called her mother.

"I hope this phone call means you've seen the light," Joyce said.

Margaret sighed. "You know, Mother, if you or Madelyn had said, 'We love you, Margaret. Whatever you decide, we'll be there to back you up, one hundred percent,' I might've *seen the light,* as you put it. But not one single member of my family seems to trust me enough or love me enough to let me come to my own decisions. You, Madelyn, the kids—all of you think you know better than I do. All of you have shown me you think I'm not capable of making a sensible choice. Even Tony thinks I'm naive."

"You are."

"Oh, for heaven's sake," Margaret cried. "Give me a break, will you?" She took a deep breath. "I didn't call to argue with you, Mother. I just called to tell you I *have* come to a decision."

"And?"

"And I've decided I'm going to continue to see Caleb, no matter what you all think and no matter what anyone says. If or when I break off with him, it'll be because I want to. Not because anyone else wants me to."

"Fine, Margaret," her mother said stiffly. "If you want to make a complete fool of yourself, I guess I can't stop you. Well, I've done my duty. I've tried to point out the folly of what you're doing. But I guess you'll have to learn every lesson the hard way. But let me tell you something, Margaret. Don't come crying to me when things fall apart. Don't expect me to help you pick up the pieces."

Chapter Twelve

For the next six weeks, Margaret spent most of her free time with Caleb. They went for long rides all over the countryside and, in early October, when the leaves became a riot of golds, scarlets and oranges, they spent a weekend camping out at Lake George.

When they spent the night together, Margaret usually stayed at Caleb's house. Although she wasn't attempting to hide her relationship with him anymore, she didn't want a repeat of the episode where Lisa had walked in on them.

The intensity of their lovemaking didn't abate. Margaret marveled at this fact. She had never considered herself a very sensual person. Certainly Anthony had never elicited those feelings. Even in the first flush of love, when she and Anthony were courting and first married, Margaret couldn't remember feeling this way.

With Caleb—Margaret blushed just thinking about how abandoned and wanton she felt. All he had to do was look at her in a certain way, and they'd be heading for the nearest bed. Margaret often wondered why this was so.

Margaret had also never laughed so much in her entire life as she had in the past two months. Anthony had never made her laugh. The things he found funny left her cold. With Caleb, even the smallest things seemed hilarious. Caleb was a great mimic, and once, after observing a rather hefty woman in a too-tight flowered dress complain to a beleaguered salesclerk, Margaret had thought she was going to have a heart attack from Caleb's exact portrayal of the woman's walk and gestures.

Caleb also made Margaret feel beautiful. It was the first time in her life she had ever felt beautiful. Oh, she had known she was attractive, in a simple, ordinary kind of way, but with Caleb, she felt really beautiful. Head-turning beautiful. He told her she was beautiful—often.

One night, when they were having dinner at a small restaurant in a little town called Ballston Spa, he said, "You get more beautiful every day. How is that possible?"

A couple of days later Rosemary said, "Magpie, romance certainly agrees with you. You're positively radiant."

The thing that pleased Margaret the most about her relationship with Caleb was the fact that there was more to it than sex, and fun, and romance.

They also talked a lot. About everything.

Caleb actually listened to her. He made her feel as if what she had to say was worth listening to. He made her feel special and smart. Anthony had always made her feel stupid.

When Margaret was with Caleb she was happier than she'd ever been. But the rupture between her and most of her family hurt. Margaret tried to pretend it didn't matter that relations with everyone except Tony continued to be strained, but it did matter. In moments of introspection, she wondered how long she would be able to stand the silent treatment she was being subjected to.

She especially missed the closeness of her relationship with Lisa. After their lunch at The Inn, where Margaret had tried to explain how she felt, Lisa had come around a little, but even though they had resumed their almost-daily phone conversations, she completely ignored the subject of Caleb, and she hadn't invited Margaret to come over for dinner or anything else. Margaret knew that several of Lisa's girlfriends were planning baby showers for her, and she wondered if she would be included in the guest list.

And then there was her youngest daughter.

Lori would call back if Margaret called the dorm and left a message for her, but she initiated no calls on her own. And when they did talk, she, too, avoided the subject of Caleb.

Madelyn completely ignored Margaret after their one confrontation. But since Margaret rarely talked to Madelyn even when they weren't disagreeing, that didn't bother Margaret.

Joyce was a real problem. Margaret had always seen a lot of her mother. Throughout the years of her marriage, she would meet her mother for lunch at least one day a week, they always saw each other at church and they spent many Sunday afternoons together, either having dinner at the Guthrie home or at Margaret's home.

All that had changed now.

All through September and October, the only times Margaret and Joyce were in each other's physical company was at church. There, for the benefit of curious onlookers, Joyce was always primly polite.

Margaret forced herself to telephone her mother every couple of days. She didn't want Joyce to be able to say that Margaret was the one who avoided her mother. But the conversations took their toll, because afterward it would take Margaret hours to shrug them off and regain her good spirits.

"I think your family will eventually come around," Rosemary said. "Quit worrying about it, Margaret."

"I wish I could believe that," Margaret answered.

Caleb also tried to reassure her. "I thought my family was going to disown me a couple of times," he said, "but they always ended up forgiving whatever it was I did that they disapproved of."

"You don't know my mother," Margaret said.

Margaret also had to suffer the knowing looks of acquaintances and the behind-her-back whispers and grins. She wondered what she'd ever done to these people, some of whom she'd actually thought of as friends, to cause them to take such glee in her fall from grace.

She and Rosemary talked about it one day.

"They're jealous," Rosemary pronounced. "Most of them have old, fat and bald husbands, and they can't stand the fact that you've snagged such a sexy stud."

If anyone else had referred to Caleb as a sexy stud in Margaret's hearing, she would have blushed to the roots of her hair, but she simply shot Rosemary a look and said, "Do you really think that's it?"

Rosemary took a bite of her tuna salad and nodded. "Yep. Sure do. Hell, I'm jealous myself." She grinned and leaned over the table. In a low whisper she said, "Come on, Magpie, you can tell me. Is he really as good as he looks?" Then she laughed uproariously as Margaret raised her fork and threatened to stab her.

Not everyone made Margaret feel like a scarlet woman, though. Sharron Centofanti, the head librarian at the Riverview Library, had been a high school classmate of Margaret's. The two had never been close friends, but Margaret had always liked Sharron, who was one of those women who didn't start to bloom until she was in college and got more attractive as the years passed.

One Thursday afternoon, Margaret stopped by the library to pick up a couple of books on origami, the Japanese art of paper folding, for a client who wanted a party with a Japanese theme. She had selected her books and was standing in line to check them out. Ahead of her was a woman she knew slightly from their mutual involvement in the band boosters' club when Lori was in the high school band. The woman's name was Shirley Polen, and after she'd checked out her books and turned to go, she noticed Margaret. Her face slid into a sly smile, and she looked Margaret up and down, then said, "It must be true what they say about young men."

Margaret could feel her face flaming. She was too stunned by the woman's audacity to answer her, and by the time she'd collected her wits, the woman was gone. Holding her head high, Margaret met Sharron Centofanti's warm brown eyes.

Sharron smiled. "Hi, Margaret."

"Hello, Sharron." Margaret's heart was still beating too fast, and she wondered if anyone else had heard Shirley's remark. She wished she could disappear.

Sharron efficiently checked out Margaret's books, and just as Margaret reached for them, Sharron leaned over and said, "Shirley's a bitch. Not everyone thinks the way she does. I, for one, am happy for you." Then she grinned.

Margaret got a warm feeling every time she thought about Sharron and what she'd said.

Toward the end of October, Lisa called one Saturday and said, "Mom, do you want to help Mary Lou and Rita make favors for my baby shower?" The two women she'd named were Lisa's best friends.

Margaret went to the work session, which took place at Mary Lou's home. Lisa even suggested that Margaret pick her up. Margaret could see that Lisa was trying to act as if nothing had happened between them, and afterward, when Margaret drove her daughter back to her house, before getting out of the car and going inside, Lisa turned to Margaret and said, "Mom, I'm trying to understand."

Margaret reached over and squeezed Lisa's knee. "I can see that, honey. And it means a lot to me. I love you, you know. I never wanted to hurt you."

"I—I know. And I love you, too. Keith and I talked about all this, and he said you're a grown woman and you always respect our decisions and that we should respect yours."

Margaret's eyes filled with tears. She leaned over and hugged her daughter, and Lisa hugged her back.

The following day, when Margaret related the story to Caleb, she felt hopeful, for the first time since the estrangement from her family began, that someday things might actually get back to normal.

Then, one morning early in November, Lisa called and said, "Mom, Keith told me he saw Lori with Sam Damato last night."

"Where? Doing what?" Margaret said in alarm. Sam Damato had a notorious reputation. The son of a city councilman, he'd been expelled from two high schools, had been accused—although the charges had been dropped—of date rape and was rumored to be a heavy drug user. Margaret, who knew his parents, had always felt sorry for them.

"Keith said they were coming out of Babycakes."

Margaret closed her eyes. Babycakes was an unsavory club where the big entertainment was topless dancing and lewd comedy.

"Keith was on his way home from an airport committee meeting, and he said by the time he realized it was Lori he'd seen and turned his car around and driven back, Lori and Sam were gone."

Margaret bit her bottom lip.

"And Mom? Lori's been skipping a lot of classes lately, too."

"How do you know that?"

Lisa sighed. "I didn't know whether to tell you or not, but when Keith told me this about Sam Damato, I thought maybe I'd better." She hesitated. "I ran into Judy the other day, and she told me. She said Lori's failing two classes that she knows of."

Margaret stared out the window. She could see her across-the-street neighbor washing his car. "I'll have to go over to the school and talk to her," she finally said.

"Yes," Lisa said. "That's why I called you. I would've tried talking to her, Mom, but you know how she is. She doesn't think much of my opinions."

She doesn't think much of my opinions, either, Margaret thought as she hurriedly showered and dressed. She considered calling Lori's dorm first, then decided against it. She would just drive over to the college and sit and wait if Lori wasn't in her room. Thank goodness, Margaret's calendar for the day was open except for a lunch date with Rosemary, and she would cancel that.

She reached the college about ten-thirty. The dorm supervisor, a crotchety old woman with pink hair, grumbled, but she let Margaret go up to Lori's room.

There was no answer to Margaret's knock, so she went back outside and sat on the low wall bordering the flower beds. It was a beautiful day, sunny and cool, with the first hint of winter in the air. Margaret breathed in the fresh air and watched a couple of squirrels frolic on the grounds. She smiled at their antics as they chased each other up and down the trunks of the silver birch trees.

She only had to wait about thirty minutes before she spied Lori coming toward the dorm. Margaret studied her younger daughter in the few moments before Lori saw her. Lori's hair was longer, and she looked like a typical college student in her tight jeans and oversize sweatshirt.

Margaret knew the exact moment Lori saw her. She stopped abruptly, then, face stiffening, she resumed walking toward her.

"Hello, Mother," she said as she drew abreast. Her gray eyes reminded Margaret of flint. There was no hint of warmth in them. "What brings you here?"

Margaret stood. "Do you have a class this hour?"

"No."

"Would you like to go somewhere and have lunch with me?"

"No."

Margaret gritted her teeth. She would not lose her temper. She kept her voice soft. "Look, honey, I know you're still angry with me, but I'd hoped—"

"Damn right, I'm still angry with you."

Margaret restrained herself from admonishing Lori about her habit of swearing. "All right, fair enough, but I'm still your mother, and I'm still paying your bills, so I think I have a right to insist you come with me. I have something I need to talk with you about."

Lori gave Margaret a look filled with daggers, but she offered no other protest and followed Margaret as she walked toward her parked car.

They didn't talk on the five-minute drive to the little sandwich shop Margaret knew Lori liked.

Margaret ordered a chicken salad sandwich and Lori ordered a bacon, lettuce and tomato sandwich. Their waiter, a boy Lori obviously knew from her smiling exchange of remarks with him, brought them their order and two glasses of iced tea, then left them alone.

Lori sat back sullenly, saying nothing.

Margaret decided she might as well plunge right in. It was obvious no attempt at conciliation would work. "Lisa called me this morning."

Lori stared at her, her lips firmly clamped shut, her arms folded against her chest.

"She said Keith saw you with Sam Damato last night."

If possible, Lori's face hardened into even tighter lines, and the look she threw Margaret was defiant.

"Sweetheart," Margaret said, leaning forward and infusing her voice with as much love as she could. "You know what kind of reputation Sam has. He's been in trouble since he was a young boy."

"What's your point?" Lori said.

Please, God, Margaret thought. Please, please help me. "My point is, Sam Damato is not the kind of person I want you to hang around with. He's bad news."

"I don't think you have any room to talk," Lori said coldly.

Pain, like a hot poker, seared Margaret.

"I mean, you're running around with the town stud, making a spectacle of yourself."

Each word pushed the poker deeper. The chicken salad Margaret had just swallowed felt like a lump in her esophagus.

Lori leaned close. Her voice dripped with venom. "Don't lecture me about Sam. If I want to go out with him, I will, and there's not a damned thing you can do about it."

"Lori..." Margaret was afraid she was going to throw up. "Why... why are you—"

"Why am I doing this?" Lori's mouth twisted into an ugly smile. "Sam's great in bed, that's why. You can understand that, can't you?"

Margaret felt numb. She felt like someone else was inhabiting her body. The only place she could feel anything was in her heart, and that felt like one great big throbbing wound. She hadn't been going to ask Lori why she was seeing Sam, as Lori had thought. She had been going to ask her why she felt so compelled to hurt Margaret. Why she seemed to hate her so much? *What have I ever done to deserve this?* she thought as Lori's angry eyes met hers.

Margaret wiped her mouth carefully with her napkin, then placed it just as carefully down on the tabletop. "All right, Lori. Perhaps there *is* nothing I can do about who you choose to spend your time with. But that's not all I wanted to discuss. I hear you're failing two subjects and skipping a lot of classes."

Lori stared at her. "Who told—"

"It doesn't matter who told me. Is this true?"

Lori opened her mouth, then shut it again.

"So it is true," Margaret said quietly. "Well, there *is* something I can do about that." She took a deep breath. "Starting today, I'd strongly advise you not to miss another class. I'd also strongly advise you to sharply curtail your social life and do some heavy studying, because if you fail even one class this semester, I won't pay your tuition or your room and board next semester. I also plan to cut your monthly allowance in half starting immediately, because as long as you're going to be spending so much time studying, you won't need money to run around on."

Two bright spots of color appeared on Lori's cheeks. She swallowed and said, "You can't do—"

"Oh, but I can, and I will." Margaret reached for her purse, removed her billfold, and extracted a ten- and a five-dollar bill. She laid them in the middle of the table. "That should take care of the bill," she said, then stood.

Lori slammed her hand down on the table, and several other diners looked curiously in their direction. "Fine," she said through clenched teeth. "Fine! Cut my allowance. Don't pay my tuition. See if I care! I don't need your money! I'll get a job dancing at Babycakes. The owner has already talked to me about it. How will you like that?"

"I won't like it at all," Margaret said quietly, ignoring the painful clutch of her heart. "But, as you so strongly pointed out, I can't tell you how to live your life. You'll have to make your own choices. However, if you start working at Babycakes, I think that will ultimately hurt you more than it will ever hurt me."

As much as she wanted to, Margaret knew she couldn't back down. She picked up her purse again. "Goodbye, Lori. I'm sorry things have to be this way."

"Where are you going? How am I supposed to get back?" Lori demanded furiously.

"Try walking. It's good for the soul."

Margaret left with her head held high. She never looked back.

Caleb knew something was wrong. Margaret had been too quiet all night. He'd made a special effort to be funny, telling her several stories about things that had happened at school that week, and she'd smiled, but he could see her thoughts were elsewhere.

She ate the dinner he had prepared with a listless disinterest, playing with the cheese-filled ravioli and only managing to get down about a third of her portion.

He hoped she'd tell him on her own what was bothering her, but when she still hadn't said anything and it was almost ten o'clock, he took her hand and said, "Meggy, what's wrong?"

She sighed heavily. She didn't pull her hand away, but she didn't return the pressure, either. "I don't know if I even want to talk about it."

"Come on, it'll make you feel better. Whatever it is is obviously bugging you. Is it your mother again?" Caleb had never met Margaret's mother, but he knew he would not like her. Even if he and Margaret were still together twenty years from now, he would never forgive her mother for the way she'd hurt Margaret.

"No, it's not Mother. It's Lori."

Lori. Caleb hadn't met Lori, either, but he knew who she was. He'd made a special point of finding out who she was and observing her from a distance. So far, what he'd seen he didn't particularly like. His personal opinion was that Lori Desmond was a spoiled little rich girl who could probably have benefited from an appropriately placed paddle when she was younger.

As Margaret told him what had happened throughout the course of the day, Caleb could feel himself getting angrier and angrier. The things Lori had said to her mother were unforgivable, he thought, and totally undeserved. A finer and more giving woman than Margaret could never be found, he was sure. Although he'd never seen her with any of her children, he knew she was a wonderful mother. Even the way she talked about her children, with that proud glow in her eye, told him so.

He found himself clenching his teeth, and he wished he could tell Lori Desmond a thing or two. Better yet, he wished he could give her a few of those well-deserved whacks.

Margaret finished by saying, "So I did the only thing left to do. I threatened her, and now I feel like a complete failure as a mother." She then tugged her hand away and covered her face. "Oh, God, Caleb," she said, her voice muffled, "what a mess my life is in."

"Meggy..." He reached for her, and for the first time since they had begun seeing each other, she resisted, shrinking away from him.

She took a ragged breath, looked at him and said, "Caleb, I'm rotten company tonight. I've got an awful headache, and if your feelings won't be hurt, I think I'm going to go home now.''

Later, as Caleb lay in bed alone, he couldn't help a rueful laugh. An awful headache. Was this the beginning of the end?

The next morning, Caleb decided that after his classes were over for the day, he would seek out Lori Desmond and try to talk to her. So the first thing he did when he reached the college was head for the administration office.

Jessie Milligan, a cute redhead who worked in the office, grinned at him. ''What can I do you for?'' she said.

''Well, since you probably won't throw over your husband and run away with me, how about looking up a student's schedule for me?''

''Oh, you,'' Jessie said coyly. ''If I said yes to your first suggestion, you'd probably run as fast as those gorgeous legs would carry you.''

Caleb laughed.

Ten minutes later, armed with a printout of Lori's schedule, he headed for his first class. His last class of the day was over at three, as was Lori's. He let his students go five minutes early, to their noisy delight, then he sprinted over to the language department building and waited outside the lecture hall.

A couple of minutes later, the students began filing out. Several of them greeted him, and he smiled and nodded, all the while watching the doors.

About a dozen students later, Lori's blond head appeared. She saw him almost immediately, and he was gratified to see the surprise she quickly disguised.

He didn't let her walk by him. He headed straight for her, touched her arm and said, "I think we should talk."

She walked quietly beside him, eyes straight ahead. When they exited the building, he motioned to a bench sitting in the middle of the Commons. "Why don't we go over there?"

She shrugged and followed him.

She sat on one end of the bench; he sat on the other.

She lifted her chin, giving him a haughty look. "So? Talk."

"You've really upset your mother," he said.

"She upset me."

"Okay, so you upset each other. But your mother's worried about you, and I'd hoped we could talk—"

"I have nothing to say to you."

Caleb had told himself to be patient, but her stubborn refusal to meet him halfway angered him. "Lori, what you're doing is stupid," he said. "Sam Damato is a punk. He'll only bring you trouble. Hell, he's brought you trouble, already. You're failing classes, you've got your mother all worried . . . But I think you know that. I think you're just trying to get back at your mother because of me."

Her eyes flashed with the first surge of emotion he'd glimpsed. "You don't know a thing about me."

"Oh, I think I do. I know you're a spoiled brat who's hurt one of the sweetest, nicest, most generous women in the world. I know you've got a mean streak and that you're vindictive and that if your mother were smart, she'd cut you off permanently or at least until you grew up."

She jumped up. "How dare you talk to me like that! You're not my father, and you have no right to say such things."

Caleb knew she was right, but he was so angry now he forgot caution. "Maybe I'm *not* your father, but one of these days I might be your stepfather."

"Not if I have anything to say about it! I don't know what your hold is on my mother, but my sister and brother and I all agree, we're going to do anything we can to get her away from you." She glared at Caleb, her chest heaving. "And let me tell you something else. You'd better watch your back, because you're right, I'm not *sweet* and *nice* like my mother. I'm also not as easily fooled."

Caleb knew he shouldn't have tried to talk to her. It was obvious he'd only made things worse.

She smiled. "You made a big mistake, buster. And you're going to be sorry."

Chapter Thirteen

That night, Caleb wouldn't see Margaret until after
nine, because she was catering a dinner meeting at one
of the downtown office buildings. She'd even suggested, when he telephoned her after his disastrous talk
with Lori, that they might skip getting together that
night.

"I'll probably be tired," she'd said. "And one of
these days we're going to have to slow down a little bit.
I mean, us being together every night must be cramp-
ing your style."

"Well, that's true," Caleb teased. "My redheaded
girlfriend has been complaining, and my raven-haired
girlfriend is threatening to commit hara-kiri."

"Seriously," Margaret said. "I don't expect you to
spend every night with me."

"Have I ever suggested that I thought you expected
it?" Caleb kept his voice light, but knew deep inside

that cracks were beginning to appear in the wall of Margaret's resolve to defy her family.

"No, but—"

"Because I don't feel that way at all. Are you trying to tell me something, Meggy? Because if you are, just say it. You don't have to beat around the bush."

"Oh, Caleb..." She sighed, the sound clearly audible over the telephone wire. "Don't pay any attention to me. I don't know what's wrong with me."

"I know exactly what's wrong with you. That damned family of yours hasn't let up for one instant. And if you ask me, that youngest daughter of yours is the worst of the bunch."

"I didn't ask you."

Caleb stiffened at her chilly reply. He told himself not to be angry. He told himself she really hadn't meant it the way it had sounded. He told himself she was just upset. It was a struggle, but he softened his voice and said, "Meggy, please, come over tonight. Let's talk about all of this. Let's see if we can't come up with something to make your life easier."

"I don't kn—"

"Please."

Another deep sigh. "Okay, Caleb. I'll be there around nine-thirty."

At nine twenty-five Caleb glanced around. He'd built a fire in the fireplace, because earlier a front had moved in from Canada, and the mercury had plunged to forty-five degrees. He'd made hot, mulled cider and had a softened wedge of Brie, a favorite paté, and some English water biscuits that Margaret particularly liked. Debussy played softly on his CD player. The drapes were drawn against the night, and his living room looked cozy and warm and inviting.

A perfect seduction scene, he thought, laughing at himself. He hadn't had seduction in mind, though, when he'd gotten ready for Margaret's arrival. He just wanted to soothe and reassure her. He just wanted her to remember that he loved her.

He wondered if she'd ever admit that she loved him, too. So far, whenever he'd said the words to her, she had only hugged him or kissed him in return. He knew she was afraid to commit herself. He had tried to figure out why, and he'd finally come to the conclusion that she wasn't so much afraid of saying she loved him, she was afraid of what this declaration would mean in terms of the future.

She was afraid of the decisions ahead of them.

And if he had a family like hers, he might feel the same way.

Hell, he told himself, you wouldn't give a damn. You'd tell them all to take a flying leap off the Empire State Building.

But it was a moot point, because he couldn't imagine his family behaving so badly. The Mahoneys were nothing if not a tolerant bunch.

Caleb wondered if it would help or hinder his cause with Margaret if he told her that lately his thoughts had been steadily turning in the direction of marriage, as he'd strongly hinted to Lori this afternoon. When he'd first thought about Margaret in those terms, it had rocked him. But in the past few weeks, the thought had gotten more and more appealing.

Still, he'd said nothing to Margaret because, for the first time since he'd been old enough to be interested in women, Caleb Mahoney was unsure of a woman's response.

Good Lord, Margaret, what have you done to me?

A little past nine-thirty, he heard Margaret's van pulling into the driveway and coming toward the carriage house. She always pulled around back, and he saw the headlights sweep the house. He walked slowly to the back door and opened it.

"Is there anything in the van you want to put in the refrigerator?" he asked as she climbed down. He'd learned early on that a caterer tried never to waste food.

"No. They ate everything. No leftovers to worry about." She walked toward him, and he saw the weary lines in her face and the smudges under her eyes. His heart twisted at this evidence of lack of sleep and worry. Once more, he wished somebody would shake some sense into Lori Desmond.

Still, Margaret looked beautiful to him. She wore a camel-colored coat over her simple navy blue dress, and as she walked past him into the kitchen, her light, fresh fragrance floated in the air.

When the door closed behind them, Caleb touched her arm, and Margaret turned to face him.

He smiled down at her, then gently drew her forward, sliding his hands under her coat. She didn't resist, but she didn't return his kiss with the eager passion he was accustomed to.

I'm losing her. He swallowed against the fear that rose in his throat. *That goddamned family of hers is winning.* Caleb wasn't used to losing anything he wanted. In his entire life, when he'd stirred himself enough to make an effort toward reaching any goal, he had achieved the desired results easily.

Jobs.

Skills.

Women.

They'd all come to him without him having to expend more than about fifty percent of his energy.

His sister Kathleen had once told him things came too easily to him. "It's cheated you, Caleb. No telling what you might have accomplished if you'd had to work hard."

Caleb knew that was true. He knew he probably could have had a successful music career if he'd cared enough about music. He knew he might have been a successful writer as well, but he'd never wanted it badly enough to do the work necessary to achieve that goal.

It was ironic, he thought, that now that he'd found something—*someone*—he cared deeply about, she was slipping from his grasp.

He led Margaret into his carefully prepared living room, settled her onto the comfortable couch and said, "I'll go get us some mugs of cider."

She nodded, her lovely eyes clouded. She gave him a halfhearted smile.

When he returned to the living room, he handed her her mug, then sat next to her. He left a foot or so between them. He knew tonight he'd have to tread softly. He didn't want those cracks in the wall to widen.

"You're worrying about Lori," he said.

Margaret nodded. She sipped her cider and didn't meet his eyes. "I just can't get the picture of her and Sam Damato out of my mind." She closed her eyes. "When she said, 'He's good in bed,' I just wanted to die. This is all my fault."

"Lord, Margaret! It's *not* your fault!"

"I appreciate your loyalty, but we both know it is. She never would have done anything like this if it hadn't been for me. For us."

"I talked to her today," Caleb blurted out.

With a stunned expression in her eyes, Margaret turned to face him. She laid her mug down on the coffee table. "You what?" she said.

Caleb sighed. He put his own mug down. "I talked to her today. I thought maybe I might get somewhere with her."

"What did she say?"

Caleb told her, leaving out the ugliest parts as well as his opinion of Lori's character. "I know now I probably shouldn't have talked to her."

"No, you shouldn't have," Margaret said, her voice strained. "You've probably made things worse. I could have told you she wouldn't listen to anything you had to say. Besides, she's my problem, not yours."

Caleb stiffened. "Well, hell, Margaret, excuse me. I thought I had a stake in this, too. I thought, as the man who loves you, that what affected you affected me. But I can see I was wrong."

She winced. "I'm sorry, Caleb. It's just that you don't know my children, so you couldn't possibly know what to say to them. And you're the cause of their anger toward me. How could you think that you talking to Lori would help things?"

"I guess I was willing to try anything to make you feel better." He reached for her hand. "Margaret," he said softly. "Let's not fight. I love you. I just want you to be happy."

She looked down. "I thought by now they might have begun to accept you. I thought things would get better. But, I don't know, they seem to be getting worse and worse."

Caleb wanted to draw her into his arms. He wanted to kiss her until she forgot about her damn family. "That's not quite true. Your other daughter and your son aren't acting like spoiled brats. It's only Lori—"

She yanked her hand away, startling him. "Lori is not a spoiled brat. She's mixed up, and she's hurt, and she's angry."

Caleb cursed himself for his tactical error. "Okay, so she's not a spoiled brat. I shouldn't have said that." He touched Margaret's shoulder, felt its rigidity as he tried to put his arms around her. "Come on, Meggy," he coaxed. "Let's forget about this tonight. Let's go to bed."

She looked up, her eyes clouded and lusterless. "That's your solution to everything, isn't it?"

Stung, Caleb dropped his hand. "I just thought maybe if we held each other—"

"That I'd forget I'm a mother? That I'd forget my responsibilities?"

"Margaret . . . come on. That's not fair. I said I was sorry. I made a mistake, okay?" But her attitude was really beginning to bug him. He'd *said* he was sorry. Was this the way things were always going to be if he crossed that invisible line she seemed to have drawn? Was she always going to shut him out of a part of her life? Maybe Kathleen was right. Maybe getting involved with a woman with grown children wasn't such a hot idea, after all. No matter how special the woman. Maybe he should just cut his losses and kiss Margaret goodbye.

As these thoughts rushed through his mind, Margaret stood. She avoided his eyes. "Caleb, I think it's best if I go home. It was a mistake to come tonight. I'm just not in the mood. I need to be by myself. I need to think."

Margaret didn't see Caleb for the rest of the week. He hadn't called her, either. She was miserable without him.

She knew he was angry and hurt. And after she got over her initial burst of anger over his ill-advised talk with Lori, she knew he had a right to be hurt.

She shouldn't have snapped at him like that. He'd only spoken the truth. Lori *was* a spoiled brat. It was time Margaret faced it. She'd done a lousy job raising her.

When three days had gone by without her hearing from Caleb, Margaret knew she would have to be the one to make the first move. She owed him an apology. He had only done what he'd done because he was concerned about her. Because he loved her.

She called him about six that evening.

"Hello, Caleb."

"Hello, Margaret. How have you been?" She heard the distance in his voice.

"Okay." She took a deep breath. "Missing you."

"Aw, Meggy," he said, his voice warmer, more like Caleb. "I've missed you, too."

"I'm sorry about the things I said. Maybe you shouldn't have talked to Lori, but I know you only did it because you care about me. Because you didn't want me to be unhappy."

"Yeah. Well, I'm sorry, too."

"Forgive me?"

"Of course, I forgive you. And I'll promise you something, too. I promise I won't interfere again."

"Thank you. And if you'll just try to be patient, give me some time, I'll try to get my family situation sorted out."

"I told you once before. I'm a very patient man."

Margaret smiled with relief. "I'm so glad you're not angry with me, anymore." She felt almost shy as she added, "Am I going to see you tonight?"

She could almost hear his answering smile. "Try to keep me away."

* * *

Thanksgiving had always been Margaret's favorite holiday. Traditionally her mother, her sister and her children and any friends they might care to invite, along with Rosemary, always came for dinner. And before the death of her father and Anthony's parents, they were part of the celebration, too.

Margaret always fixed a huge turkey and made her grandmother's recipe for old-fashioned bread dressing. Rosemary always brought the wine and flowers for the table. Joyce always baked pumpkin pies. Madelyn contributed fresh fruit salad. And the past couple of years, Lisa had done the fresh vegetables and dips for starters.

This year Margaret dreaded the holiday. She almost wondered if she should just suggest to Caleb that they go away somewhere. She knew he wasn't planning to join his family's Thanksgiving gathering because he was going to New York over the Christmas holidays and would spend time with them, then. He'd even dropped hints about her going with him to meet them.

Margaret wasn't sure how she felt about that. But right now she couldn't worry about it. Right now she had to decide what to do about Thanksgiving.

"Mother!" Lisa said when Margaret called her later that day and tentatively suggested she and Keith might like to spend this Thanksgiving with Keith's parents. "Not have Thanksgiving at your house! Why, it wouldn't even *seem* like Thanksgiving somewhere else."

"Oh, all right, it was just an idea. I'll have it here. Don't worry. I just thought, with Lori and the way she feels about me right now..."

"If Lori doesn't want to come, that's her problem," Lisa declared.

No mention was made of Caleb, and Margaret wondered if this was Lisa's tacit way of saying she was finally ready to meet her mother's lover.

But what about Margaret's mother? And Margaret hated the thought that Lori would be alone. But what could Margaret do? She wasn't going to back down from her stand with Lori. She couldn't.

Don't be such a coward, Margaret. You've made your choice. There's nothing wrong with your choice. Now let your family make theirs.

Yes, Margaret thought. Unless she wanted to hurt Caleb's feelings, possibly irreparably, by not inviting him, she would probably have to force a showdown.

And in this corner, she thought, we have Margaret, who has led the life of a wimp, but has now put on the boxing gloves, albeit reluctantly, and in that corner we have Margaret's family, most of whom are much better equipped for a long bout than she is.

She finally brought up the subject with Caleb.

He smiled. "I think it's time," he said enthusiastically. "Maybe when your family all meet me, they'll realize I'm not so bad."

Don't bet on it, Margaret thought. "I doubt Lori will come."

He grimaced. "Have you heard anything from her?"

"No. Lisa told me that one of her friends told her that Lori hasn't started working at Babycakes, though." This had been an enormous relief to Margaret. "Instead she's taken a waitressing job at Magazine's." Magazine's was a local Italian eatery popular with the college crowd.

"Are you going to call her to invite her for Thanksgiving?"

"It wouldn't do any good. She won't talk to me when I call. I thought I'd just write her a note telling her no matter what's happened between us, that I love her, that I want her here with us. Let her know the door is always open."

"Are you going to tell her I'll be there?"

"I think I have to."

"Look, Margaret," Caleb said. "I'm a big boy. My feelings won't be hurt if you really don't want me at the Thanksgiving table. Maybe I should stay away and just let Lori—"

"No," Margaret said. "I've decided, and that's that. You're coming." She reached up to kiss him. "I don't think Lori would come, anyway, even if you weren't going to be there, and as long as the rest of my family is there..."

But when Margaret called her mother, Joyce said, "I've accepted an invitation from the Needhams. You remember the Needhams, don't you?"

Margaret refused to let her mother know how much she'd hurt her. "Well, it'll seem very strange without you, but I hope you have a good time."

"A lot of things seem strange lately," Joyce said.

And when Margaret called Madelyn, her sister said, "Oh, I'm going skiing in Stowe with the Stricklins that weekend. Sorry, Margaret."

Okay, thought Margaret. So that's the way it's going to be. Well, as far as she was concerned, it was their loss, not hers. The rest of her guests would have a wonderful, stress-free day without the dampening influence of her mother and her sister.

She put off calling Lisa again to tell her that Caleb would be joining them, though. She knew it was cowardly of her, but she couldn't seem to help herself. She finally could stall no longer, and called her daughter a couple of days later.

"It's only fair to tell you Caleb is coming for Thanksgiving, too," Margaret said. "I hope this won't make a difference."

"Oh," Lisa said.

"I really want you to meet him, honey." Margaret tried not to sound as if she were begging.

"Well..."

"I think, if you'll just give yourself a chance, you'll like him."

"Well, I guess I *should* meet him."

Margaret breathed a sigh of relief. She crossed her fingers and sent up a silent prayer. If Tony, and now Lisa, would accept Caleb, it might not be long before Lori would, too. And if Margaret had her children in her corner, she would be able to withstand anything her mother or sister dished out.

The Tuesday before Thanksgiving, Caleb called her early in the day to say he was going to be tied up that night. "I know I was supposed to come over, but something's come up."

"That's okay. What's going on?"

"They've called a special hearing about the proposed airport." He chuckled. "You know, the one your friend Floyd Hubbard wants so badly."

"He's not my friend. He's Lisa's father-in-law."

Caleb chuckled again. "Yeah, I know he's hot for your body."

Margaret ignored his joking and said, "Why are you going to the meeting? I didn't know you were involved in this issue."

"I haven't been, but this is the final hearing before the state zoning commission. They're supposed to make a decision tonight. And Jake Byo—you know, I've told you about him—well, he's been involved from the beginning, and he twisted my arm. Said they really need me. He said I'm more eloquent and can help them state their case better.''

Margaret ignored the uneasy feeling in the pit of her stomach. Not only Floyd, but Keith as well, had a lot to lose if the commission ruled against the airport. "This seems like an odd time to have a hearing," she said instead. "Right before the holiday starts.''

"Yeah. I think the airport committee called it now on purpose. I think they're hoping that the opposition, a lot of whom come from the university, will be out of town.''

Margaret toyed with the idea of asking him not to go. What would Keith think if he saw Caleb there, heard him arguing against the airport? But she discarded the idea as soon as it formed. She had no right to tell Caleb what to do in this respect. So all she said was, "Okay. Talk to you tomorrow, then.''

"I could come over later," he said.

"No, Caleb. I need to get a good night's sleep. *And* get up early. Remember? I told you. I've got a luncheon to cater tomorrow as well as all the preparations for Thanksgiving here on Thursday. No, you go on to your meeting and then go home.''

"Boy, you're getting bossy," he said.

At ten minutes past eleven, the telephone rang.

Margaret, who had just gone to bed, grabbed it on the first ring, heart pounding. The phone never rang late at night unless something awful had happened.

"Mother?''

"Lisa? Honey, what's wrong?''

Lisa's voice shook.

"Omigod," Margaret said. "It's not the baby—''

"No. It's not the baby. It's that, that *boyfriend* of yours.''

"Caleb?" Margaret's heart stopped. Had something happened to Caleb?

"Yes, your precious Caleb! Did you know he was going to the airport hearing tonight?"

"I, uh . . . yes . . . he mentioned it."

"Well, he made a *fool* out of Keith's father in front of everybody at the meeting."

"Oh, dear . . ."

"And now the State Zoning Commission has ruled against the airport. Floyd and Dolly are furious. You should have heard them. You should have heard the things Floyd said about you! And I didn't know *what* to say. And now Keith is really upset and he said I don't need this. Not now. Not when it's so close to my due date." She started to cry.

"Oh, honey, I'm sorry, but Caleb—"

"Don't make excuses for him, Mother. I didn't call to listen to you defend him. I just called to say one thing. If that man is going to be there Thursday, we're not coming."

"Darling—"

"You decide, Mother. Then let me know." She hung up.

Margaret replaced the receiver very quietly after Lisa broke the connection. She stared into space.

It was no good.

Her family would never accept Caleb.

She had been kidding herself. She had thought eventually things would work out. But now it was clear to her that she would have to choose.

Her family.

Or Caleb.

She could not have both.

Chapter Fourteen

All day Wednesday Margaret agonized over her decision.

How could she give Caleb up?

Even the thought made her feel sick to her stomach.

And yet, how could she reject her child? And her coming grandchild?

Oh, if only someone else would make the decision for her. Tell her the right thing to do.

She knew she had to make up her mind by six o'clock, because Caleb had promised to come over then to help her with her Thanksgiving preparations.

At six o'clock, her time had run out.

When Caleb walked in, he took one look at her face and said, "What is it, Meggy?"

"Sit down, Caleb," Margaret said. "Do you want a beer or a glass of wine or something?"

Caleb took off his dark blue wool sport coat, draped it over a chair, then sat at the kitchen table. He shook his head. "Tell me first."

Margaret sat across from him. She folded her hands together to keep them from shaking and looked at him. He always looked wonderful to her, no matter what he wore, no matter what he was doing. Today he had on a white, cable-knit sweater over a pale blue shirt and jeans. His dark hair, always worn a bit too long, curled over his collar. His blue eyes were somber as they met her gaze.

Now that it was time to put her decision into words, she wasn't sure she'd be able to say it without crying. She didn't want to cry. This was going to be hard enough without going to pieces in front of Caleb. "Caleb, I...I—" She stopped. *Oh, God. Why is life so hard?*

Caleb frowned, watching her, then slowly, comprehension settled into his eyes.

Margaret took a ragged breath. "I can't see you anymore." She could feel the tears coming, and bit her bottom lip to stop them.

He nodded slowly, his eyes never leaving hers.

Why didn't he say something? Margaret couldn't look at him anymore. She ducked her head. "I—I'm sorry, Caleb. This hasn't been an easy decision."

"No, I'm sure it hasn't," he said quietly.

Margaret fought to get her emotions under control. "I just...I just can't deal with this anymore," she finally said, looking up again.

"What prompted this decision?"

"Lisa called last night, all upset about what happened at the airport hearing. She said you made a fool out of her father-in-law, and I guess she and Keith were subjected to a tirade against both you and me afterward."

He grimaced. "Oh. I never thought about that."

No, Margaret thought sadly. She knew he hadn't. She guessed this episode had really pinpointed the basic difference between them. If their positions had been reversed, Margaret would have immediately realized how going to that meeting, standing up and opposing Lisa's father-in-law, would put additional strain on the relationship between Margaret and Lisa. Margaret would not have gone. Caleb, being Caleb, had simply gone blithely on his way.

"Lisa said if you were coming to dinner tomorrow, she and Keith were not. She told me to choose."

He nodded again. "And you have."

"Yes. I—I don't see what else I can do." Wasn't he going to argue with her? Wasn't he going to tell her all the reasons she was wrong?

He cleared his throat and pushed his chair back. "Well, Margaret..." He stood, lifting his coat and putting it on. "I'll respect your decision. I'm really sorry you feel you have to do this, but I won't put more pressure on you. I think your family has done enough of that."

Margaret felt as if her heart had lodged somewhere up inside her throat, and she couldn't breathe. She pushed her own chair back and stood.

They looked at each other for a long moment, and Margaret tried to tell Caleb with her eyes all the things she had never been able to say out loud. She tried to tell him she loved him, and if things were different, she would have been happy to be with him forever. She tried to tell him how sorry she was and how miserable she knew she was going to be. She tried to tell him how much the past months had meant to her and how she would remember them for the rest of her life.

Most of all she fought to keep the tears from falling.

And then he gave her a little half smile, walked around the table and put his hands on her shoulders.

Margaret swallowed against the pain. She could feel the tears, and she knew if Caleb didn't leave soon, she would break down and blubber like a baby.

He touched the tip of her nose with his finger. "Goodbye, Mrs. Desmond," he said softly, his blue eyes filled with regret. "It was great while it lasted."

Margaret wasn't sure she'd make it through the day. Somehow she'd managed to get the turkey into the oven at eight that morning, even though she'd spent a completely sleepless night and had cried for hours. She'd awakened with the worst headache she'd ever had, and when she looked into the bathroom mirror, she moaned.

Tony and Darcy had arrived about eleven, all smiles. Margaret genuinely loved Darcy, who was pretty and a bit plump and had dark laughing eyes and even darker curly hair. She was good for Tony, who had a tendency to be a little too much of a worrywart because he took after Margaret. Darcy kept him loosened up, and Margaret knew she made him happy. That alone would have been enough to make Margaret like her.

Margaret tried hard to pretend everything was fine, but when Tony said, along about twelve o'clock, "What time is your friend, the professor, coming?" Margaret was hard-pressed to keep her voice steady when she answered, "He's not."

"He's not? Why not? I was looking forward to meeting him. Darcy was, too, weren't you, Darce?"

"Yes, I was," Darcy said.

Margaret thought about saying something innocuous, then changed her mind. She met Tony's topaz eyes, the exact shade of hers, and said, "Listen, I'd rather not talk about it right now. Let's just say it was a choice between Lisa and Keith coming or Caleb coming, and I chose your sister."

Tony frowned. "Gee, Mom, I'm sorry."

"It's okay," Margaret said hurriedly, knowing it was never going to be okay.

Lisa and Keith arrived at one, and right on their heels came Rosemary, who looked gorgeous in a kelly-green pants suit and matching bowler hat.

"Very sexy," Tony said, hugging Rosemary.

"Very sexy, yourself," she said, laughing at him.

Margaret got her guests settled in the living room and excused herself to check on dinner.

Rosemary followed her out to the kitchen. "What's going on? I thought Caleb was going to be here."

Margaret opened the oven and lifted the foil covering the turkey. It looked done and she picked up a two-tined fork to test it. "He's not coming."

"Why not?"

Margaret finished poking the turkey and turned off the oven. She straightened, meeting Rosemary's quizzical gaze. "I'll tell you about it some other time, okay?"

Rosemary's forehead wrinkled in concern, but all she said was, "Okay."

Somehow Margaret got through the day. They ate and drank and talked, and she did her bit as the hostess, but all the while, she kept thinking, *I'm never going to see him again. I'm never going to see him again.*

She didn't know how she was going to stand it.

* * *

Caleb threw some clothes into his car and blew town Thanksgiving morning. He didn't know where he was going, and right then, he didn't care.

He ended up in Atlantic City, and he spent the day at the blackjack tables.

He spent the night at the craps tables.

The following morning, seven hundred dollars poorer, he collapsed into his hotel room bed and slept for the next nine hours.

Friday night he got up and went out to dinner. After eating, he went back to his hotel and thought about hitting the tables again, but he knew that would be stupid. Instead, he packed his few belongings and drove back to Riverview.

On Saturday he found himself driving past Margaret's street, and when he realized what he was doing he got mad at himself and went home and played his fiddle for hours.

On Sunday he celebrated his thirty-eighth birthday alone by drinking an entire bottle of champagne and eating a fully loaded sixteen-inch pizza.

When his parents and various sisters and brothers called to wish him many happy returns, he cracked jokes and pretended everything was wonderful.

Everything was terrible, but there didn't seem to be one damned thing he could do about it.

Monday morning, between classes, he caught a glimpse of Lori Desmond in the distance. She didn't look much happier than he felt, and for about two minutes, he was glad. Then he realized what an immature thought that was, and he castigated himself.

On Tuesday, driving on Main Street, he saw a woman who looked like Margaret. His heart hopped up into his throat, and he slowed down as he passed by.

It wasn't her.

For the rest of the day he thought about living in Riverview and running into her occasionally. He thought about maybe seeing her with another man, because a woman as vibrant and beautiful and giving as Margaret would surely date again. There would be someone her family would think suitable for her, eventually.

Could Caleb stand that?

On Wednesday, he picked up the phone and called the dean of the English Department at Columbia. "I'm ready to talk," he said.

The following week he gave his notice to his boss.

Margaret missed Caleb more than she'd ever thought it would be possible to miss another human being. She felt as if a part of her had been cut out and left a huge, gaping hole that she'd never be able to fill. This had been a terrible year. First Anthony, who despite his faults and their problems, had died, and that had shocked and saddened her. And now Caleb.

For days after that fateful Wednesday before Thanksgiving, she was constantly on the verge of tears. A customer was rude to her one day, and afterward Margaret cried for hours.

She couldn't eat, and she couldn't sleep.

She lost weight.

She knew she'd done the only thing she could do. She wasn't a woman who could give up everything for love. Her family, her children, her coming grandchild, her good name—all were too important to her.

She told herself that in this life we cannot have everything. She reminded herself, as she'd reminded her children all of their lives, that everything comes with a price tag. Sometimes the price for what we want is too high.

Margaret knew this misery could not last forever. A part of her would always miss Caleb, but eventually, she would get over this heartsickness.

The second week of December, when Margaret settled down to read the Sunday paper, she saw the write-up of his friend's wedding accompanied by a picture of the wedding party. Her gaze latched onto the photograph, and tears welled in her eyes as she devoured Caleb's beloved face.

She should have been at that wedding with Caleb. A few weeks earlier, right before their breakup, he had mentioned it to her, saying, "I've been wanting Jake and Marilyn to meet you. I think you'll like them, and I think they'll like you."

Margaret closed her eyes and let the tears come. *Oh, Caleb, Caleb, I miss you so.*

At night, Margaret would lie in bed and it would take her hours to fall asleep. This was the first time in her life she'd ever had a problem sleeping. But her body missed Caleb. It missed the loving and the sweetness and the comfort being near him had brought to her. She ached for him, and some nights she wasn't sure she could endure it.

But what was her alternative?

By the third week of December, with the imminent arrival of Lisa's baby, Margaret finally began to feel better. She woke up one morning and actually smiled as she thought of the day. She was picking Lisa up and they were going shopping for the remaining items Lisa needed for the baby. *I think I'm going to make it,* she thought. *I'll never forget Caleb, but I think it's going to be all right.*

Three days later, she stood next to Keith in the birthing room and watched as the tiny head of her granddaughter emerged. A few minutes later, when Keith handed Margaret the tiny wrapped bundle, and Margaret gazed at the baby's perfect little face, her heart filled with an incomparable love, and she was sure that the worst was definitely behind her.

Caleb read about the birth of Margaret's granddaughter in the "Riverview Ramblings" column. He thought about sending her a congratulatory card.

Quit acting like a high school kid. Leave her alone.

He wondered if she ever thought about him. He wondered if she ever lay in bed at night and ached for him the way he ached for her. Things had gotten so bad, he'd actually picked up the phone to call a former girlfriend, then he'd changed his mind.

He didn't want just anyone.

He wanted Margaret.

Instead he poured himself into strenuous physical activity, something he'd usually avoided. Caleb had never understood why anyone liked to sweat. Personally he hated it. But now he ran every morning, pushing himself to go farther and faster each day. He started going to a local gym and he worked out every night.

It was ironic, he thought, looking at himself in the mirror as he stepped from the shower one morning, that physically he looked better than he'd ever looked, and there was no one to appreciate that fact except him.

He wondered how long it would take before his first and last thoughts of the day centered around something besides Margaret.

He also wondered if there was anything he could have done differently. One night, when he and Jake ate dinner together at a local pub, Caleb actually broke down and told his friend the entire story.

"I think some things are destined to happen and others aren't," Jake said. He motioned to the waiter. "Bring us a couple more beers."

"Yeah," Caleb agreed glumly.

Caleb was glad he'd decided to take the job at Columbia. Once he was away from Riverview, he would be able to put all of this behind him. He counted the days until he would leave. It was only four days until his Christmas vacation started, and he was planning to spend about ten days of it in the city. Then he'd come back to Riverview, pack up his belongings and get moved a few days after New Year's. Then mid-January he would start his classes at Columbia.

He told himself that once he was in his new environment, he would be okay. He would forget Margaret. Gradually she would be just a sweet memory.

Caleb spent the ten days of his Christmas trip sharing his brother's apartment in Soho. He visited old friends and spent a lot of time at his parents' place in the Bronx. A couple of years ago, when his father retired, his parents had taken their life savings and his retirement fund and plunked it down on a small house.

There were always people coming and going from their house. Other retired cops who liked to chew the fat, as they called it, with Dennis Mahoney. Would-be singers who paraded in and out of the tiny cubbyhole Siobhan Mahoney had claimed for her students' voice lessons. Neighbors and friends and their grown children and their children's friends. Cousins and aunts and uncles and assorted hangers-on. It never changed, Caleb thought as he looked around.

Christmas Day was filled with lots of food and drink and people and noise. Caleb watched it all, not really feeling a part of it, but not really feeling sad or lonely, either. He did find himself wishing Margaret could be here. He knew she would have enjoyed his family, and he'd bet they would have loved her.

He returned to Riverview the Thursday before New Year's, which fell on Saturday this year. A weird kind of sadness gripped him as he drove down Revere Street. In just a week he would be gone. He'd never see this pretty little town again, he was sure of it. And Margaret. He would never see her again, either.

Don't think about it. There's nothing you can do to change things, so put it out of your mind and get on with your life.

The next day he spent in his office at the college, packing up all his books and papers. Then he went home. It was the first time he'd ever spent a New Year's Eve at home—alone. He'd been invited to two parties—one at Jake and Marilyn's place and another given by an ex-girlfriend. He'd declined both invitations. He just didn't feel like making conversation and being entertaining.

About eight that night he sent out for some Chinese food and ate it out of the paper cartons while watching a movie on cable. When the show was over, he shut off the TV and picked up John LeCarré's newest book.

He couldn't concentrate. He kept thinking about the movie, one of the best he'd ever seen. He kept thinking how Slade, the protagonist, had loved women and had admitted that his dream was to wake up beside the same woman every morning.

We all want someone to love. Someone who loves us.

Caleb put his book aside. He got up and walked to the front window. There were lights on in the main house. He wondered what his landlords were doing tonight. Were they toasting each other with champagne in front of the fireplace?

What was Margaret doing tonight?

Was she at a party somewhere?

Dancing with someone, maybe?

A vision of her face, laughing up at him when they'd danced at the old mill, filled his mind. He could still feel her satiny skin and smell her light, flowery fragrance. He could still remember how her hair, so soft and silky, had felt against his cheek.

Meggy.

He closed his eyes. If only he could see her again. Just once.

At that very moment, Margaret stood at the fringes of the well-dressed crowd in Rosemary's vaulted-ceilinged living room and wished she could go home. She decided that as soon as midnight was over with, she would leave. She'd leave sooner, but she was afraid Rosemary would be mad at her.

It wasn't Rosemary's fault Margaret wasn't having a good time. As New Year's Eve parties went, this was a very good one, but Margaret was having a hard time keeping her mind off Caleb this evening.

Maybe it was the dress she'd worn—the same black one she'd worn the night he took her to the old mill and they'd had such a magical, romantic evening.

Maybe it was just that a person should welcome in a new year with someone they loved.

Maybe it was simply that she was feeling sorry for herself.

Whatever the reason, Margaret was miserable. She thought about the past couple of weeks. She'd managed to convince herself she was doing fine, especially after the birth of little Krista. And as long as Margaret's days and nights were filled with helping the new mother, she actually believed this. But after Christmas, when Lisa no longer needed much help, Margaret had had to really look at her life; she knew things were far from wonderful.

Her relationship with her mother had still not gone back to normal, and Margaret wondered now if it ever would. That really wouldn't bother her that much, but the situation with Lori did. Lori had spent her holidays with Judy's family and had stubbornly refused to participate in any of her own family's Christmas activities. She wouldn't even come to see Lisa's baby unless Margaret wasn't there.

Margaret's business didn't give her much satisfaction right now, either. In her most honest moments, she knew that she could walk away from her business tomorrow and never miss it.

Even her euphoria over the birth of her granddaughter had evaporated. Krista was Lisa and Keith's daughter—their responsibility. No matter how much time Margaret spent with the baby, Krista could not fill all the empty places in Margaret's life.

Margaret grimaced. Empty.

She thought about how she hated going home to that empty house. Funny that the house hadn't seemed so empty after Anthony died, even though they'd lived together for so long. Yet now that Caleb was gone, it felt cavernous.

Margaret could hardly stand to be there by herself, which was really why she'd let Rosemary talk her into coming to this party.

She glanced at her watch. Only about ten minutes until midnight.

What was Caleb doing now? Was he laughing and flirting and making up limericks? Was he dancing and having a good time? That he was with others, Margaret had no doubt. She couldn't imagine Caleb sitting home by himself. Not on New Year's Eve. He'd probably had several invitations to choose from. Maybe he'd even attended a couple of parties already.

Although she rarely let her mind go in this direction, she wondered if he would end the evening with someone. Take someone home to his bed. The thought hurt so much, she hurriedly shoved it away. She couldn't stand to think of Caleb with another woman, to imagine his hands touching someone else, bringing her to those glorious peaks . . .

Stop it! Stop torturing yourself!

A few minutes later, when Rosemary passed out party hats and horns, Margaret listlessly took hers. When the clock struck midnight, she blew her horn, smiled and said, "Happy New Year." She even allowed herself to be kissed by a couple of the men who made the rounds, laughingly kissing every woman at the party.

She felt ridiculously close to the edge of tears and knew she had to get away before she made an absolute fool of herself.

A few minutes later she saw her chance. Rosemary had disappeared in the direction of the kitchen, and no one else was paying any attention to her. Trying to be inconspicuous, she slipped into Rosemary's guest bedroom, unearthed her mink from the pile of coats on the bed, walked out into the hall and tried to open the front door and slip out without anyone noticing.

She'd almost made it when Rosemary came up behind her and said, "Oh, no, you don't! Did you think you were going to leave without saying goodbye?"

"I'm sorry. I didn't want to take you away from your other guests."

"Why are you leaving so early? I was just going to serve coffee and my famous cheesecake."

"I'm awfully tired. Please don't be mad at me, but I just want to go home."

Rosemary gave her a sympathetic look. "It's all right. I watched you tonight. I know you were miserable. I'm not going to force you to stay. But gimme a hug first, okay?"

Margaret almost cried then. She could feel the tears wanting to come. She blinked and hugged Rosemary hard. "Thanks for being such a good friend, Ro," she said. "Happy New Year."

"Happy New Year, Magpie. Drive carefully."

Margaret walked out into the cold, starry night. There'd been a heavy snowfall the day before, and because of it, the night seemed brighter than usual. In the distance, she could hear firecrackers popping.

Was this the way the rest of her life would be? she wondered. Going home alone to an empty house and an even emptier bed?

She allowed the tears to come as soon as she reached the safety and darkness of her car. She hadn't cried in weeks, but tonight the hot tears slid down her face and she didn't try to stop them.

Oh, Caleb, when will I ever forget you? Why can't I forget you? Why does everything seem so meaningless without you?

She drove slowly and it took her about five minutes longer to reach her subdivision than normal. She turned onto her street. Most of the houses still had lights burning. Several had bunches of cars parked in their driveways and nearby. Through the big picture window in Betty Flack's house, she could see a party going on.

When Margaret reached her house, she pulled into her driveway, hitting the remote before she was halfway to the garage. She entered the garage, opened her door and got out of the car.

She walked toward the house.

Out of the corner of her eye, she saw something. Someone.

In the shadows.

Her heart slammed into her chest, and she gasped.

And then he walked forward, into the light from the garage. "Meggy?"

Now her heart leapt. "Caleb?" she whispered. Then she said, "Caleb!"

For one long moment, they stood there, looking at each other. Then he opened his arms, and she walked right into them, lifting her face for his kiss.

Chapter Fifteen

He kissed her again and again.

Margaret's head spun, and in her mind, the only thought was, *Caleb, Caleb.*

The garage light went out, plunging them into darkness, and it was only then that Caleb said, "You've been crying." He held her face between his hands and peered down at her. In the moonlight, his eyes looked like dark pools. "Why?"

"I missed you," Margaret whispered.

"Oh, God, Meggy," he said, pulling her close and holding her head against his chest. His voice was ragged. "I missed you, too. I thought I'd get over missing you, but I haven't. I thought I could leave Riverview without seeing you again, but I couldn't. Are you angry that I came?"

"No. I'm glad." She tried not to think about the words, *leave Riverview.*

"I love you, Meggy," he murmured, stroking her hair.

For a long moment, Margaret let him hold her while she absorbed his touch, his smell, his words. Then, silently, she pulled away and, taking Caleb's hand, led him to the back door.

She fumbled with her key, and he said, "Here. Let me."

There was no need for words. Once they were inside the house, they just walked to the stairwell, climbed the steps and went into the guest bedroom. In the darkness, they quickly undressed. Together they pulled down the spread and climbed into the bed.

Seconds later, they were burrowed under the blankets and Margaret was wrapped in Caleb's arms.

She trembled as his hands found each place that had ached for him over the past weeks.

He moaned as her hands glided over his body, remembering, reacquainting, reigniting.

And when he entered her, pushing deep, she wanted to cry again, but this time because all the empty places had been filled.

Later, lying close together, Caleb murmured, "I forgot to wish you a Happy New Year." He kissed her nose. "Happy New Year, beautiful Meggy."

"Happy New Year, Caleb."

He stroked her hair. "I love you."

Margaret sighed and tightened her arms around him. "I love you, too." She felt his smile against her forehead.

"That's the first time you've ever said that," he whispered. He kissed her hair.

"Yes." A great sadness filled Margaret. Admitting her love for Caleb wasn't something that would make things easier for her. "But it doesn't change anything, Caleb. Tonight, well, tonight was—"

"Don't say tonight was a mistake."

"No, not a mistake. But it . . ." Margaret swallowed. *Oh, God, don't start crying again!* She took a deep breath, willed herself to be strong. "It can't keep happening. I haven't changed my mind, or anything. Besides, didn't I hear you say something about . . . leaving Riverview?"

"Yes, I'm leaving on Wednesday."

Pain exploded in Margaret's chest. "S-so soon," she said before she could stop herself.

"Come with me, Meggy. Come with me. We belong together. Surely you can see that. Let's get married and go to New York together."

Margaret started to cry. She wanted so badly to say yes. To say goodbye to her old life, to the old Margaret, to all the problems and responsibilities and other people's expectations and demands. But how could she? How could she? She would be saying goodbye to her children. To her grandchildren. The girls especially would never forgive her. Never. "I'm sorry, Caleb," she said. "I wish I could be the kind of woman you want me to be, but I can't."

Caleb held her until her tears stopped. For a long time he said nothing. Then he raised her head and kissed her mouth lightly. "I guess this really is goodbye, isn't it?" he said, and Margaret heard the resignation and acceptance in his voice.

When he left the bed, Margaret didn't try to stop him. He dressed quickly. Just before he turned to leave, he said, "You won't hear from me again. For my own peace of mind, I'm going to cut you out of my heart. I have to if I want to survive."

And then he was gone, and Margaret knew she wouldn't have to try to cut him out of *her* heart. Her heart would never be whole again.

For the next few days, Caleb hoped against hope that Margaret would change her mind. Each time the phone rang he hoped it was her, but it never was.

By Tuesday he knew it was finally, irrevocably, over. He did his final packing, and about midnight, tired and resigned, he went to bed.

At one o'clock, the phone rang. Caleb, who had been lying in bed awake, picked it up immediately. He didn't even have time to wonder who would be calling so late.

"P-Professor Mahoney?" said a muffled female voice.

"Yes? Who is this?" He sat up and turned on the bedside lamp.

"Th-this is Lori. Lori Desmond."

Margaret's daughter? Alarm widened Caleb's eyes. He could hear soft sobbing. "Lori? What's wrong? Has something happened to your mother?" Fear, thick and metallic, clogged his throat.

"No. It's not my mother. I—I'm in trouble. C-can you come and get me? I—I wouldn't have called you, but I didn't know where else to turn."

A thousand questions raced through Caleb's mind, but all he said was, "Where are you?"

"I'm...I'm out on Old Market Road." Her voice was steadier now. "I'm in the phone booth near that boarded-up filling station."

Caleb frowned. What in the hell was she doing out there? Especially this late at night? "It's going to take me at least twenty minutes to get there."

"I—I'll be waiting by the phone booth."

As he drove, too fast, to the location she'd given him, he knew Lori Desmond was in some kind of trouble. Bad trouble. But why had she called him?

When he approached the spot she'd said she'd be waiting at, his headlights picked her up. She was huddled on the frozen ground, sitting with her back against the phone booth. When he slowed the car, she got up, and Caleb was shocked to see that her face was bruised. Blood had dried under her nose, and one eye was puffed up. He couldn't see her clothing because she clutched a dark down coat around herself.

He opened the passenger door, and she climbed in.

"What happened?" he said. "Were you in an accident?"

"Can I tell you about it on the way?" Her voice was subdued.

Caleb nodded and turned the car around. "Where are we going? To the hospital? To your mother's?" He peered at her again. She looked as if someone had beaten her up.

"No!" Lori said, panic edging her voice. "I—I thought, I *hoped,* you'd take me to your place."

"I don't think that's a g—"

"Please, Professor Mahoney. *Please.*"

He heard her desperation and even though he wanted to say, *"No way,"* he said, "And then what?"

"I...I just need to get cleaned up before anyone sees me. I don't want anyone to know about this."

Caleb decided rather than argue with her, he would take her to his place, and then he could call someone to come and get her.

"Why me?" he said.

"Y-you're the only one I could think of who might help me without telling my mother." She put her face in her hands and began to cry. "I d-don't want her to kn-know how stupid I am."

When they reached the carriage house, Caleb saw how she winced as she got out of the car. But when he tried to help her, she shook her head and said, "No, I'm okay."

Inside the house, Caleb got a good look at her. She kept her coat wrapped tightly around her, but her face looked terrible. "Someone beat you up," Caleb said. "Who was it? Sam Damato?"

Lori nodded, eyes bleak.

"Son of a bitch," Caleb swore. "I'm going to have to call the police. You know that, don't you?"

"No!" Her gray eyes beseeched him. "No, please, please don't do that! I . . . it was all my fault. I should have known better." Tears streamed down her face.

"How could it be your fault that you got beaten up?"

"Could I please get cleaned up first? Then I'll tell you everything."

Caleb ran his fingers through his hair. What should he do? "Okay," he said, "I've got some antiseptic and stuff." He led her into the bathroom and rummaged around in the duffel bag he'd packed earlier. When he found what he needed, Lori finally relinquished her coat. Once she did he saw why she'd clutched it around her so protectively. Her green silk blouse, which had probably been expensive, was torn. There were no buttons left on the front of it, and underneath, he saw an ugly bruise on her shoulder.

As he worked on her face, she sat quietly. He knew it must hurt, but all she did was wince a couple of times. She was a brave little cuss, he thought.

When he finished with her face, he told her he'd shut the door and she could clean the rest of herself up. "I'll find you something else to wear," he said.

Ten minutes later, she emerged from the bathroom with her hair combed and dressed in her own jeans and one of Caleb's sweatshirts. Her eye had started to discolor, and Caleb knew by morning it would be a real beaut. There'd be no way she could keep what had happened to her a secret, not unless she planned to hide out for a week or so.

For the first time, Lori seemed to notice all the boxes. "Are you going somewhere?"

"Didn't you hear? I took a job at Columbia University. The movers are coming at eight tomorrow morning."

Lori shook her head. "No. I—I haven't been spending that much time at school lately."

"I think I can find a couple of mugs, though. Let's go out to the kitchen, and I'll make us some coffee, and we can talk."

She followed him to the kitchen and sat down. Caleb fixed them each a mug of instant coffee, then sat across from her. "Tell me about tonight," he said.

She shrugged, the gesture full of defeat. "It's just your normal, ugly story," she said wearily. "We were out at this party in Johnsonville, and on the way home Sam scared me because he was driving so fast. I said something about slowing down, and he got furious. He slammed on the brakes, and I wasn't wearing my seat belt, and I hit the dashboard. I started to cry, and he called me a stupid bitch, and he, well, he started to hit me and yell at me. He scared me because he was acting so crazy. I—I... somehow, I managed to get the car door open, and I jumped out." She raised anguished eyes to Caleb's. "I was afraid he was going to come after me, but he didn't. He just took off and left me there, about a mile away from where I called you."

Caleb's fists had clenched halfway through her story, and now his teeth were clenched, too. He thought about how much he'd like to punch Sam Damato in the face. "Lori, that creep needs to be put behind bars."

"Oh, God. Don't ask me to call the police. I just can't stand people knowing how stupid I was."

"Do you want him to keep doing this to other women?"

"No, of course not!" Her gray eyes showed the first real flash of passion he'd seen tonight.

"He will."

She nodded and bit her bottom lip.

Caleb watched her struggle to make a decision. "Let me take you home to your mother," he said softly.

Lori looked at him. A lone tear slid from her right eye. "Sh-she despises me."

"She loves you."

Lori shook her head. Several more tears followed the first one.

"She *does* love you, believe me." When she continued to shake her head, he said, "She broke up with me because of you and your sister. She couldn't stand the thought that she'd made you so unhappy."

"Sh-she won't want to see me."

"Yes, she will, and she'll help you do whatever needs to be done."

Lori gave one long, shuddering sigh, then finally nodded. "Okay."

Caleb drove her to Margaret's house. He parked in front. "I'm not going in with you," he said. "I'll wait until she comes to the door, then I'm leaving. And Lori?"

"Yes?"

"I'd rather you didn't tell her I brought you home."

"But why?"

"I just think it's better that way." Caleb didn't want Margaret's gratitude. He wanted her love.

When the doorbell rang in the middle of the night, Margaret rushed downstairs, sure some catastrophe had befallen someone in her family.

When she saw Lori on the doorstep, she nearly had a heart attack. A dozen emotions rushed through her. "Lori," she said. "Oh, my God, what's happened to you?"

Twenty minutes later, Margaret gathered her wayward youngest daughter into her arms, and they held each other for a long time.

"M-mom, can you ever forgive me?" Lori said later. "You were right all along. And I was so stupid!"

"Oh, darling," Margaret said around the lump in her throat, "of course, I forgive you. I love you. Nothing you could ever do would make me stop loving you."

"I love you, too," Lori said. "And I'm so sorry for everything."

Then Margaret said, "Now it's time to call the police." Smiling encouragingly at her daughter, she picked up the phone.

The movers were late. Caleb felt antsy, and he wished they'd hurry and get there. Last night's events had shaken him, and he wanted to get away before he yielded to temptation and did something stupid.

Jake stopped by at eight-thirty. "Movers haven't shown up yet?"

"Nope."

"Movers are always late," Jake said as if he were an authority on the subject.

"I'm gonna miss you, old buddy."

"Just make sure you get a two-bedroom apartment so Marilyn and I can come and visit often."

Caleb laughed. "I can tell you don't know anything about New York if you think I'll be able to afford two bedrooms." He squeezed Jake's shoulder. "I'll let you two have my bedroom. I'll sleep on the couch."

Jake hung around a few more minutes, then, with an offhand shrug, gave Caleb a hug. "Good luck," he said in parting.

The movers showed up at nine.

By ten o'clock they'd loaded everything of Caleb's into their van, including his bike, and pulled off down the driveway.

Caleb stowed his two small bags in the trunk of his car, took one last look at the carriage house and climbed into the Miata.

Ten minutes later, as the sign proclaiming Riverview, Population 21,324, disappeared from view, he whispered, "Goodbye, Meggy. Have a good life."

As the weeks of January crept by, Lori's bruised body slowly healed. She and Margaret made the mutual decision that she wouldn't return to school this semester. Lori said she'd like to find a job and stay at home until summer, then make some decisions about her future.

Margaret agreed. She gave her youngest daughter a lot of tender, loving care. They talked a lot, and Margaret could see that out of the bad had come some good. Lori seemed so much more mature, so much more ready to try to understand her mother and her point of view.

And Margaret tried to be just as understanding and receptive to Lori's feelings.

One day, at the end of the month, the two of them were sitting at the dinner table, and Lori said, "Mom? Can I ask you something?"

"Sure, honey."

Lori fiddled with her wadded-up napkin. "Why did you and Professor Mahoney break up?"

At the mention of Caleb's name, Margaret's heart contracted. She tried never to think of him. She couldn't stand thinking of him, because then the pain became unbearable. She turned her head, because she didn't want Lori to see the pain she knew was reflected in her eyes.

"Mom?" Lori said softly.

Margaret kept her head averted. "It—it just didn't work out." Tears blurred her eyesight. *Oh, God. Please. Please.* She hadn't cried since the night he left. She couldn't allow herself to cry. If she did, she might never stop. "I—I don't want to talk about it." She forced the tears away, forced her voice into a false lightness. Laughing slightly, she said, "I thought you'd be glad. You didn't like him at all."

Lori shrugged, her eyes thoughtful. "Maybe I was wrong."

Margaret swallowed and looked away again. What she would have given to hear Lori say those words months ago.

"Mom?"

Margaret turned, met Lori's gaze. Her daughter's gray eyes held a peculiar expression.

"He—he's the one who brought me home that night."

Margaret stared at Lori.

"I know I told you I called a friend, but it was him."

"But why? Why Caleb?"

"I was ashamed to call any of my friends, and I thought I couldn't call you or Lisa. He was the only one I could think of."

Caleb! Caleb had gone out there, seen Lori, taken care of her, brought her home to Margaret. And for weeks Margaret hadn't known. Hadn't even been able to say thanks.

"If it hadn't been for him, I'd've never come home. He told me you wouldn't be mad. He told me you loved me."

Margaret's throat was too full to speak. She stood, and with her back to Lori, walked to the sink. Leaning against the counter, she fought the tears. But she couldn't keep them away. She could feel her control slipping. Feel her tenuous hold on herself dissolve. *Caleb, Caleb.* Finally she bowed her head and quit fighting.

She felt Lori's hands on her shoulders. "Mom, Mom, please don't cry."

And then they were crying together. "Mom, I'm sorry. I'm sorry I was so awful. You love him, don't you? You broke up with him because of us. Because of me."

Later, after Lori had gone to bed, Margaret sat in the rocking chair in her bedroom. She thought for a long time. She thought about Lori's last words, after they'd talked for hours.

"Why don't you call him?" Lori said.

"I can't."

"Why not?"

"Because I'm sure by now he never wants to hear from me again."

"How do you know unless you try?"

How do you know unless you try?

The next morning, Margaret left the house before Lori awakened. Lisa got up early now, and she knew her oldest daughter would already be in the throes of her morning routine.

Lisa grinned when she saw Margaret. "Hi, Mom! You're just in time to see Krista take her bath. And this is really weird, that you should come over this morning, because I was going to call you later, anyway. There's something I wanted to talk to you about."

"There's something I wanted to talk to you about, too," Margaret said.

They waited until after the baby was bathed and settled in Margaret's willing arms. As she fed Krista her bottle, Lisa said, "What did you want to talk about?"

"Why don't you go first?" Margaret suggested, wanting to put off the moment of truth just a little bit longer.

Something similar to uncertainty slid into Lisa's green eyes. "Well...okay." She swallowed. "I...uh, wanted to tell you about something that's happened. Keith, well, you know, he hasn't been too happy working for his father."

"Really? I didn't know that."

"Yeah, well, I didn't want to say too much, because you know, Keith felt kind of disloyal, but his father's kind of hard to take sometimes."

What an understatement, Margaret thought.

"Anyway, Keith's been putting out feelers for other jobs and, uh, he's gotten an offer he really wants to take."

"Why, that's wonderful, Lisa!"

Lisa bit her lip. "I'm not sure you'll think so when I tell you where it is."

"Where is it?"

"London."

Margaret's eyes widened. "London? You mean, London, England?"

"Uh-huh."

Margaret just stared at her daughter. Myriad emotions rushed through her mind.

"Say something, Mom."

"I'm speechless."

"I know this is a shock to you. It...it was a shock to *me*."

"London," Margaret said again. "My goodness..."

Lisa's face broke into a tentative smile. "You mean, you're not mad?"

"No, honey, I'm not mad. If you go, I'll miss you terribly, of course, but I'm not mad."

"I told Keith if you were too upset, we couldn't go."

Margaret smiled. It warmed her heart that Lisa was so concerned for her feelings. And as much as she wanted to say, don't go, she knew she couldn't put that kind of burden on her daughter. "Of course, you must go if Keith wants this job. Lisa, sweetheart, as much as I'll miss you and Keith and the baby, you...you have your own life to lead." *Just as I have mine.*

They talked for a while, and Lisa told Margaret all about the offer. Krista finished her bottle and fell asleep, and Lisa took her from Margaret and put her in her crib. They stood looking down at the sleeping baby, and Margaret thought about life and how it continued to march on. She thought about change and growth and the natural order of things.

When they walked into the kitchen again, Lisa said, "Mom, there's something else I've been wanting to talk to you about."

"What's that, honey?"

"Are...are you happy?"

When Margaret didn't answer immediately, Lisa said, "I've been thinking about this lately. Thinking how maybe we were unfair to you."

Margaret smiled. "Well, as a matter of fact, that's kind of what I wanted to talk to *you* about."

After leaving Lisa's, Margaret headed straight for her mother's house. She hoped Joyce would be home, because now that Margaret had made her decision, she wanted to take action. And before she could take action, she had to settle things with her mother.

Joyce answered the doorbell, only a flicker of surprise lighting her eyes. "Hello, Margaret," she said coolly.

Margaret stamped the snow off her boots and walked into the foyer. She removed her coat and handed it to her mother, then carefully removed her boots. She knew how Joyce hated her house getting tracked up.

Joyce led the way into the living room, and Margaret suppressed a smile. Before Caleb, when Margaret came to visit, she and her mother always sat in the family room. Only company ever sat in the living room. Margaret guessed she'd now been relegated to that status.

"What brings you here this morning?" Joyce said.

Margaret met her mother's gaze levelly. "I wanted you to hear this from me."

Her mother's expression didn't change. "Hear *what* from you?"

"I'm leaving for New York in the morning. I don't know if Caleb will still have me, but if he will, I'm going to marry him."

Under her makeup, Joyce's face turned red. "You're going to *what?*"

"I believe you heard me, Mother."

"You really *have* lost your mind."

Margaret shrugged. "It's my mind to lose."

Joyce's eyes narrowed. "I really hate it when you become flippant, Margaret."

"And I really hate it when you dismiss decisions you don't agree with by insulting me and calling me names." Margaret couldn't believe how good it felt to say the things she'd been wanting to say for so many years.

Joyce stood, her face furious. "I don't know what's happened to you. You're not the daughter I've known all these years."

"No, that's true. I'm not, thank God. I've finally discovered some backbone. I've finally realized that I can't please everyone. And I've finally come to understand and accept that no matter what I do, it will never be enough to make you love me."

Joyce stared at her.

Now Margaret stood, too, and watched a multitude of emotions play over her mother's face. She fought the sadness for what could have been. "There was a time when I hoped that someday things might be different between us, but now I know they never will be." Then she closed the distance between them, leaned over and kissed her mother's cheek. "Goodbye, Mother," she murmured. "I love you, but I have to live my life the way it's best for me."

It hadn't been difficult to get Caleb's address. Margaret had simply called Jake Byo, Caleb's friend, and within minutes, the address and phone number were securely tucked into her purse.

She left for New York at eight the following morning. She wasn't brave enough to drive into the city, so she parked her car at the train station in Albany and caught the ten o'clock train.

With all the stops and starts, she didn't arrive at Grand Central until four that afternoon. A half-hour taxi ride later, she stood across the street from Caleb's apartment building and tried to get up the courage to go ring the bell.

She had never been so scared in her life.

What if he said it was too late? She wouldn't blame him if he did. Maybe he had decided it was a good thing she hadn't taken him up on his offer. Maybe he had already cut her out of his heart, as he'd said he was going to, and found someone else.

What would she do if that were the case?

Die. That's what she'd do. Die.

Oh, come on, quit being so melodramatic. You're not going to die. Besides, how could you feel worse than you've been feeling?

That was true, Margaret thought.

As she stood there, torn by indecision and plagued by her doubts, the door to Caleb's building opened, and Margaret, heart knocking madly, stared.

Caleb, followed by a pretty, dark-haired young woman, came out of the building and down the front steps. He looked wonderful, Margaret thought, even as her heart contracted painfully, because Caleb put his hands on the young woman's shoulders, said something to her, then kissed her cheek. She grinned up at him, and they both laughed. Then she turned, waved, blew him a kiss and walked off.

Margaret watched him watching her go. She wanted to move, wanted to run away, but her legs seemed frozen in space. One thought hammered away in her brain. She'd blown it. She'd blown her chance for happiness with Caleb. It was too late. He *had* found someone else.

She knew she would feel the pain later. Now her only awareness was the cold and undeniable knowledge of the death of her hopes.

Taking one last look at Caleb, she turned and walked away.

Caleb was still smiling at his sister's parting remark. There was no one like Kathleen for raising his spirits. For some reason, the last few days had been tough ones. Margaret had been on his mind again, and no matter how many times he told himself he was a fool to keep thinking about her, he hadn't been able to cut her out of his heart, as he'd so valiantly told her.

He shoved his hands into his pockets and crossed the street. Looking up, he saw a woman several yards away, walking rapidly in the same direction. Something about her caused his heart to skip a beat.

God, you're really in a bad way if you see Margaret in every woman on the street.

But, damn, she really *did* look like Margaret. She wore a long black wool coat and black boots. He'd never seen Margaret wear an outfit like that, but that didn't prove anything. Her hair was the same color, and she had the same kind of walk.

He sped up, closing the distance between them.

When she reached the end of the block, she turned right, heading west, and for one second, before the building on the corner obscured his view, the afternoon sun lit her profile, and Caleb's heart stopped.

"Meggy!" he shouted. He began to run.

Margaret heard Caleb call her name, but she didn't stop. His footsteps pounded behind her.

"Meggy!"

She finally stopped, wishing the earth would open and swallow her up. *I can't do this, I can't.* She prayed that God would give her the strength to endure the next few moments.

Slowly she turned to face him.

"Meggy, what are you *doing* here?" he said. He frowned. "Has something happened?"

She shook her head. The lump in her throat was so big, she wasn't sure she could talk.

He clamped his hands on her shoulders and searched her face. "What is it?"

Margaret finally found her voice. "Nothing. I shouldn't have come."

"Why *did* you come?"

"It doesn't matter."

His eyes blazed with blue fire. "Dammit, Margaret. Will you *talk* to me?"

Margaret couldn't meet his eyes. She didn't want to see the pity she knew would be there. "Please, Caleb, just let me go."

"No! Dammit, will you look at me?"

Slowly Margaret lifted her gaze.

He stared at her. "Meggy?" he said softly. "Why did you come? Have you changed your mind?"

Margaret blinked back her tears. She nodded. "I'm sorry. I—I know it's too late."

"It's *not* too late!" he shouted. A slow smile spread across his face. "You came to say you'd marry me?"

She nodded again. Hope flickered inside her.

"Oh, Meggy!" He threw his arms around her and lifted her up, twirling her around and yelling, "She's going to marry me! She's going to marry me!"

"Caleb, put me down," Margaret said. "People are staring at us." Happiness spread over her like a warm blanket.

"New Yorkers wouldn't be caught dead staring," he said, laughing. "Besides, who cares?" He set her down, then kissed her soundly, and Margaret's heart soared. "Oh, God, I love you."

"Oh, Caleb, I love you, too."

He kissed her again, and Margaret wound her arms around his neck and gave herself up to the wonderful feelings. When they broke apart, Caleb's eyes were shining. "C'mon. Let's go back to my place where we can have some privacy." He put his arm around her shoulders, and they walked back to his apartment.

Once they were safely inside the third-floor walk-up, Caleb enfolded her in his arms again and kissed her for a long time. When he finally let her up for air, he said, "Now, before I make mad, passionate love to you, tell me everything."

Margaret smiled. "First tell me who that girl was."

He frowned. "What girl?"

"The one you kissed on the sidewalk."

His frown slid into a wide grin. "Maybe I *won't* tell you. Maybe I'll just keep you guessing."

"Caleb," Margaret said threateningly.

"It was my *sister*. Now are you happy?"

"Your sister?" Margaret couldn't remember when she'd ever felt so completely happy. She grinned. "Your sister."

"Yep. The infamous Kathleen. You'll love her. She's great." He took her hand and led her to his leather couch. He put his arm around her and drew her close. "Now will you tell me everything?"

Margaret began by telling him about her conversation with Lori. She watched his face carefully when she told him about Lisa and Keith moving to London. She didn't want him to think this was the reason she'd changed her mind.

"I'd already decided what I was going to do before Lisa told me," she said.

He searched her face for a long moment, then he smiled. "I believe you."

Margaret could feel her body relaxing.

A little later, Margaret said, "Caleb, one thing is bothering me."

He kissed her forehead. "What?"

"We've never talked about children."

"What about children?"

"I—I can't give you any."

"Really?" he said in mock surprise. "I thought you were giving me three. Plus a grandchild. Geez, a grandchild! If I'm gonna be a grandfather, I'd better get my act together, don't you think?" He chuckled.

"Oh, Caleb, are you sure you don't mind? I mean, most men want children of their own."

He hugged her close. "Meggy, sweetheart, I've never been so sure of anything in my life."

Much later, lying in bed with Caleb and feeling totally and completely at peace, Margaret said, "How would you feel about Lori coming to New York this summer and living with us for a while? It wouldn't be for very long, maybe just a few weeks."

He never hesitated. "Fine with me."

"I told her if she wanted, she could transfer to NYU."

"Sounds great. She'll love NYU."

"That's where she's always wanted to go, you know. They've got a terrific drama department."

"I know."

"I love you, Caleb."

"I know that, too."

Still later, Margaret said, "You know, you've never made up a limerick about me."

"Hmm. That's true."

"Well, come on. Make up one."

He chuckled. "You're a slave driver, aren't you?"

A few minutes later, he said, "I love a woman named Meggy, who's beautiful, sexy and leggy." For emphasis, he slid his hand over her thigh.

Margaret batted his hand.

"When she smiles and sighs, and looks deep in my eyes, I feel almost as rich as Carnegie."

"Almost as rich!" Margaret teased.

"Okay. Okay. Richer than Carnegie."

"That's better."

"No, *this* is better," Caleb said, and then proceeded to show her what he meant.

* * * * *

THE PARSON'S WAITING
Sherryl Woods

A life of harsh assignments had hardened
correspondent Richard Walton. Yet his heart yearned
for tenderness and warmth. He'd long ago given up
the search for these precious qualities—until town
parson Anna Louise Perkins entered his life. This
courageous, loving woman's presence could be the
cure Richard's soul so desperately sought....

Don't miss THE PARSON'S WAITING,
by Sherryl Woods, available in September!

She's friend, wife, mother—she's you! And beside
each Special Woman stands a wonderfully
special man. It's a celebration of our heroines—
and the men who become part of their lives.

Don't miss **THAT SPECIAL WOMAN!** each month—
from some of your special authors! Only from
Silhouette Special Edition!

**Silhouette Books
is proud to present
our best authors, their best books...
and the best in your reading pleasure!**

**Throughout 1994, look for exciting books
by these top names in contemporary
romance:**

DIANA PALMER
Enamored in August

HEATHER GRAHAM POZZESSERE
The Game of Love in August

FERN MICHAELS
Beyond Tomorrow in August

NORA ROBERTS
The Last Honest Woman in September

LINDA LAEL MILLER
Snowflakes on the Sea in September

*When it comes to passion,
we wrote the book.*

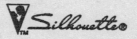

Silhouette

SPECIAL EDITION™

THE Jones GANG

by Christine Rimmer

Three rapscallion brothers. Their main talent: making trouble. Their only hope: three uncommon women who knew the way to heal a wounded heart! Meet them in these books:

Jared Jones

hadn't had it easy with women. Retreating to his mountain cabin, he found willful Eden Parker waiting to show him a good woman's love in MAN OF THE MOUNTAIN (May, SE #886).

Patrick Jones

was determined to show Regina Black that a wild Jones boy was *not* husband material. But that wouldn't stop her from trying to nab him in SWEETBRIAR SUMMIT (July, SE #896)!

Jack Roper

came to town looking for the wayward and beautiful Olivia Larrabee. He never suspected he'd uncover a long-buried Jones family secret in A HOME FOR THE HUNTER (September, SE #908)....

Meet these rascal men and the women who'll tame them, only from Silhouette Books and Special Edition!